"And what are you going to do about it?" she asked boldly.

Ian put his arms around her waist. "Something I've wanted to do for a while now...."

Tilting his head slightly, he kissed her. It was slow and deliberate, gentle without being too soft, and firm with conviction.

The kiss was more than enough to get Mackenzie's attention. She felt light on her feet and giddy. Caught up in the moment, she felt her arms make their way around Ian's neck. She didn't want this moment to end.

Ian didn't, either, as he held her tighter and opened his mouth to take in more of hers. Mackenzie was happy to give in to his urgency, as hers was just as demanding. The kiss seemed to go on and on and her body temperature rose. Mackenzie wasn't sure she could ever remember another time she was kissed like this. The man definitely knew what he was doing.

Books by Devon Vaughn Archer

Kimani Romance

Christmas Heat
Destined to Meet
Kissing the Man Next Door

Kimani Arabesque

Love Once Again

DEVON VAUGHN ARCHER

is dedicated to writing heartwarming, soulful and passionate romances.

Devon had the distinction of becoming the first male to write solo for Harlequin's Arabesque line with the groundbreaking 2006 contemporary romance *Love Once Again*. The novel went on to become number one among the Top Ten African-American Stories in eHarlequinNews.com.

Devon's heartwarming holiday love story *Christmas Heat* marked his debut romance novel for Kimani Romance, reaching number four on eHarlequin's Top Ten Holiday Reads list.

Devon lives in the breathtaking Pacific Northwest with his beautiful wife, Loraine, and is busy at work on his next Kimani Romance novel, *Christmas Diamonds,* due out in November 2009.

Devon encourages fans to join his growing group of friends on his MySpace page, www.myspace.com/devonvaughnarcher.

Kissing
the
Man
next door

DEVON VAUGHN ARCHER

KIMANI
ROMANCE

For all those ladies out there who believe that the love
of your life could be as close as right next door!

Also to the very special women in my life:
H. Loraine, Jacquelyn, Marjah Aljean
and my lovely nieces, Kendre and Keeare.

 KIMANI PRESS™

ISBN-13: 978-0-373-86115-6
ISBN-10:   0-373-86115-X

Recycling programs
for this product may
not exist in your area.

KISSING THE MAN NEXT DOOR

www.kimanipress.com

Printed in U.S.A.

Dear Reader,

Following the wonderful time I had writing my last Kimani Romance novel, *Destined to Meet*, I am now delighted to bring you *Kissing the Man Next Door*.

In this novel, hairstylist and lounge singer Mackenzie Reese is on her own again after her teenage son, Ryan, makes the decision to live with his father on the other side of the country.

When handsome radio disc jockey Ian Kelly moves into the house next door, it doesn't take long for sparks to fly. But just as these sparks begin to turn into all-consuming flames, Mackenzie learns that Ryan may be returning home after all. This could put the brakes on her new relationship with Ian, who never placed fatherhood too high on his list of priorities.

Can Ian get along with Ryan? Will the romance he shares with Mackenzie continue to sizzle?

Sometimes neighborly love can be the best kind of love in the air!

I hope you enjoy *Kissing the Man Next Door*. And make sure to stay tuned for my next Kimani holiday-season novel, *Christmas Diamonds*, coming in November 2009.

Readers can join my friends list on MySpace at www.myspace.com/devonvaughnarcher.

Also visit my Web site at www.rbarriflowers.com/DevonVaughnArcher.html.

Best,

Devon Vaughn Archer

Chapter 1

Mackenzie Reese decided to do the neighborly thing and introduce herself to the man who had just moved in next door. Never mind the fact that she'd been good friends with the previous occupants and missed them deeply. If not for a job transfer overseas, Joelle and David Schofield would still be living there now. But they weren't anymore and she would just have to deal with it.

Mackenzie wouldn't pass judgment on the new homeowner, at least not until she met him. She'd only gotten a glimpse of the man so far. She estimated he was at least six-four—six inches taller than she. His head was shaved bald and he had a black mustache with just the slightest hint of hair on his chin.

He also had a yellow Labrador, though Mackenzie was not especially fond of dogs these days. There had been too many times when some neighborhood dog had managed to get into her flower garden. Once she'd had the gate to her backyard

fixed, there hadn't been any more problems with dogs, and
Mackenzie intended to keep it that way.

There was no indication that her new neighbor had a wife
or children.

Would he send for them once things were set up? Mackenzie had also noted that his silver BMW had Connecticut
license plates.

So what brings him to Cheri Village, Vermont?

She could think of any number of things in this growing
town not far from Burlington, and probably would be wrong
on every one. It was best not to speculate. She supposed he
would spill the beans in due time if they ever became friends.

Mackenzie had no problem making new friends. It was relationships she had trouble with. After a failed relationship
with her college sweetheart, James, and then yet another with
a cheating husband, Brent, she had pretty much sworn off
men. Most were more trouble than they were worth. Her
neighbor was probably no exception to the rule, even if he was
single and available.

*Besides, the man probably wouldn't like a woman with a
child, anyway.*

Mackenzie had a fifteen-year-old son, Ryan, who had
recently decided to live with his father and stepmother in
California. It had been the last thing Mackenzie had wanted,
as she loved Ryan more than anything and felt she'd done a
good job raising him all by herself. He was the one good thing
to come out of her failed marriage and she would never have
sent him away if it had been up to her. But it was Ryan's
choice and she believed he was at a stage in his life where he
needed a strong male role model to help guide him in the right
direction. Her personal issues with Brent aside, she knew
Ryan's father could do that.

This had unexpectedly given Mackenzie more freedom to

live her life as a long-distance mom and single woman. As a thirty-seven-year-old with two careers, she had lots of pent-up passion and pleasure to give to the right man, should he ever come along.

Mackenzie moved up the blue cobblestone walkway in her mules toward her neighbor's two-story Adirondack-style home. It had red cedar siding and a shingle roof, giving it a rustic feel. There was a turret on each corner, plenty of windows and a burnt sienna wraparound porch. She glanced over at her own Cape Cod–style house with its gray stone exterior, a white slate roof and side gables. Built in the early twentieth century, Mackenzie considered it a historical treasure, though she welcomed the renovations the home had undergone over the years.

Mackenzie could hear the dog barking as she stood at the fiberglass door. Sensing it was on the other side and in no mood to be friendly, she actually considered coming back another time. Then the door opened.

Expecting to see the dog licking its chops, she instead found herself face-to-face with its owner. He was every bit as tall as she imagined, if not taller. The man was solidly built and wearing a formfitting crew-neck shirt and jeans.

Quite handsome, too.

"Hi," she said, managing to find her voice. "I'm Mackenzie Reese, your next-door neighbor. Just thought I'd stop by and welcome you to the block."

"Kind of you to do that." The man smiled broadly, causing Mackenzie to feel as though she'd melt on the spot. "Ian Kelly."

He put out a hand and she shook it, noting his hand was surprisingly soft. For one desperate moment, she wondered how that hand might feel on her body.

"Nice to meet you, Ian," she managed to say, willing her voice to remain steady.

"Likewise. I've been meaning to drop by your place to introduce myself, but I keep getting tied up with one thing or another—"

"That's okay," she said. "We're all pretty busy these days."

Ian twisted his lips. "Yeah, I suppose so. It's still no excuse not to be neighborly."

"I promise not to hold it against you." Especially when she was at least as guilty in not stopping by sooner.

He grinned. "Glad to know. I'd hate to get off on the wrong foot right off the bat."

Mackenzie laughed. "Baseball analogy. Interesting." Could he be a professional athlete?

"Bad habit of mine when it comes to getting to know someone."

"I'd say both feet are solidly on the ground as far as I'm concerned," she told him.

Ian gave an amused chuckle. "I can already tell that we're going to get along just fine."

"Is that what your crystal ball is telling you?" Mackenzie teased him.

"Actually it's more my gut instincts and seeing what's right in front of me."

"Hmm…" She was unsure how to top that.

There was a pause as their gazes met. Mackenzie felt an intense heat radiate from his stare. He had deep, gray-brown eyes that did not blink.

Ian broke the silence, frowning. "Where are my manners? Do you want to come in?"

Though tempted to see what the man had done with the place now that it was his, Mackenzie checked herself. "Maybe some other time. I have to get to work."

He gave her a look of disappointment, but quickly recovered. "That's cool. I was about to take Otis out for a walk anyway."

She cocked her brow. "I take it Otis is your dog?"

He grinned sexily. "Yeah. He gets antsy when he's stuck inside for too long."

"Don't we all," she couldn't help but say. *Just be sure to keep him from tearing up my yard and we won't have any problems.* "Well, I'll let you get to it. See you around."

"Count on it," Ian responded as though he knew something she didn't.

Ian Kelly watched with more than a little interest as his attractive neighbor sashayed away. He'd been checking her out from afar since he'd moved in, but hadn't been prepared for this up-close look. She was all that and then some.

Tall and slender with just the right curves and bends, she was wearing a coral shirtdress that seemed as though it were made for her body. He liked her shoulder-length, brunette hair. It was brushed back, layered and parted on the side. It went well with her high cheekbones and square face. He guessed Mackenzie was in her mid-thirties or just a few years under his forty.

He'd noted that she wasn't wearing a wedding ring. *So she is single, too.* And there was no indication that she had any kids. Another good sign. The last thing he was looking for was to become a daddy for the first time. Not that he had an issue with children, per se. He simply wasn't willing to take on that responsibility right now.

Ian definitely liked what he saw in Mackenzie. She was certainly a far cry from his last neighbor in Westport, Connecticut. While seventy-five-year-old Sarah Mae Stevenson was the most likeable person in the world, almost like a mother to him, she wasn't quite what he had in mind for exploring his romantic fantasies.

However, Mackenzie just might be. Something told Ian she

would be able to keep up with him under the sheets every step of the way. The very notion gave Ian an adrenaline rush—one he hadn't felt in a while.

Had his neighbor really been able to have such a powerful effect on him in just a couple of minutes? Or had he gotten carried away with his imagination?

The fact was he'd never been able to settle down for one woman. That was because he hadn't met someone who could really capture his attention for very long. But if Mackenzie was half as interesting inside as she was sexy outside, perhaps he would be singing a different tune this time around.

Ian went to get Otis, whom he'd reluctantly put in a downstairs bedroom so as not to intimidate his visitor. The dog was truly harmless, but there was no reason to get off on the wrong foot with someone who might not be comfortable with dogs. He opened the door and the Lab jumped up on him as if reuniting with a long-lost friend. Ian felt the dog's wet tongue graze his chin lovingly.

"Sorry about that, boy. I didn't want you to scare the poor lady to death with your brand of affection. Give her time and I know you'll have her eating out of your hands."

Ian watched the dog race out of the room and down the hall. There was plenty of room for him to roam inside. That had been one of the main selling points of this house. Another plus was the incredible view of the Green Mountains. The Lamoille River was practically at his beck and call. Then there was the proximity to the resort town of Burlington. It offered an easy escape for fun and frolic outside of Cheri Village.

He considered it an added bonus that his next-door neighbor was a real hottie. Ian wondered just how long it would take to get to know her better.

Chapter 2

Mackenzie was still thinking about her encounter with Ian when she got to work. She didn't expect to be impressed by the guy next door, but there was no getting around the fact that Ian Kelly was a sight to behold—broad featured, fit and tall enough to be able to handle a woman like her. He was all man and he made Mackenzie wonder why she'd waited so long to introduce herself.

But even that wasn't enough for her to fall all over the next-door neighbor. Assuming he didn't already have a lady, she wouldn't allow herself to get too carried away after one brief meeting anyway.

Why don't you see if a friendship develops before trying to get the man into bed?

Mackenzie walked through the doors of Magnificent Hair Salon, which she co-owned with her best friend, Sophia Rockford. They had bought the salon three years ago and now had a staff of six hairstylists. It was the perfect place to be for the latest hairstyles and clients were guaranteed to leave with a smile on their faces.

Sophia, a tall and slender ex-model, greeted her. "So, I see you finally decided to show up."

Mackenzie cocked a brow. A quick glance at her watch revealed she was actually half an hour ahead of opening.

"Did we have an earlier appointment that I forgot?"

Sophia laughed. "Nope. Just messing with you, girlfriend. You're never late."

Mackenzie flashed a humorless smile. "I try not to be."

"Hey, I was wondering, did you ever get up the nerve to check out your new neighbor?"

Did I ever. Mackenzie blushed at the thought and wondered if Sophia, who seemed to have more men than she could count, had mental telepathy.

"I met him today."

"And…?" Sophie looked at her. "Do tell."

"We barely said more than hello and goodbye," Mackenzie replied, wishing she'd had more time to converse.

Sophia batted her eyes. "And I'm supposed to believe that?"

"Why wouldn't you?"

"Because I know you, and there's always a lot more words than that to pass through those pouty lips. Particularly when trying to make a good first impression."

Mackenzie's mouth dropped. "Who said anything about making a good first impression?"

"Well, you certainly didn't want to make a bad one, did you?" Sophia asked.

Mackenzie cracked a smile, wondering why she even bothered with Ms. Snoop. "In this case it wasn't about impressions," she tried to convince herself. "All I wanted to do was welcome the man to the block."

"I'll bet you did just that."

Mackenzie fluttered her lashes. "Meaning?" *Why am I being so defensive?*

"Meaning nothing other than I'm sure you made him feel like he belonged."

"Not sure I would go that far," Mackenzie said. "I did what any good neighbor would do—introduced myself. End of story."

"Or beginning of one."

Mackenzie held her tongue, wondering if in fact this might be the start of a good friendship or more.

Sophia looked at her polished nails. "Well, at least you broke the ice."

"It was never that chilly between us." In fact, she found the opposite to be true, feeling the heat from Ian as though he had breathed fire at her.

"Well, that's a good sign. What does he look like? Is he single?"

Mackenzie laughed. "Sounds as if you're auditioning the man to play a leading role in your love life."

Sophia tossed back her blond-and-burgundy Senegalese twists. "And what if I am?"

A wave of jealousy gnawed at Mackenzie. She and Sophia had never competed for a man before. Though both were divorced, it was Sophia who had expressed her freedom through various male conquests. Mackenzie preferred to focus much of her time working on customers' hair and her part-time gig as a lounge singer. When at home, she liked to work on her flower garden and catch up on reading. And of course, she enjoyed the precious time she spent with Ryan.

Men were not part of the picture these days.

But that could change with Ian, assuming Sophia didn't set her sights on him.

"Then he's yours!" Mackenzie said, hoping Sophia wasn't serious.

Sophia wet her glossy lips. "I don't think so. I've got my hands full right now trying to decide if Alfonso or Derrick have what I'm looking for. I'm just trying to get the 411 on the man to see if he might be right for you."

Mackenzie was happy to hear that, though in the end she had to decide for herself if a man was worthy of her attention.

"Well, he's gorgeous. He's tall, bald and muscular. He has a nice mustache. Need I say more?"

"Sounds like a real catch." Sophia batted her lashes. "And no wife or girlfriend in the picture?"

"Not that I've seen. Of course I haven't exactly asked him about his love life."

"Guess you'll find out soon enough one way or another."

Mackenzie chuckled. "I'm really not planning to start dating my next-door neighbor. Right now I'd settle for just getting along with him and his dog."

"What type of dog?"

"A Lab, I think. Why?"

Sophia met her eyes. "Getting to know a man's dog and the particulars of its species is the best way to get to know the man himself."

Mackenzie arched a brow. "And just when did you acquire this knowledge?"

"Since I started seeing a man with a cute Dalmatian that seems to be the center of his life."

"Maybe you need to let him go?"

Sophia twisted her lips. "Or maybe you'll find that your neighbor's Lab just might become woman's best friend."

Mackenzie couldn't help but smile at the notion. Fortunately, she was spared any further suggestions when the first customer of the day walked into the salon.

* * *

"Hey, Mom," Ryan said to Mackenzie on the phone two days later.

"How are things going there?" she asked hesitantly. She half expected him to complain about everything and anything, but so far it had been just the opposite each time he called. He seemed to get along well with his stepmother and had made new friends. Then there was the fact that he was in Los Angeles and able to enjoy the year-round sunshine and see his favorite team, the Lakers.

"It's cool."

"Really?" She could breathe normally again.

"Yeah. I'm really starting to settle in here."

"I'm happy to hear that." More than he knew. When Ryan had told her he wanted to live with his father, Mackenzie thought it was a reflection on her as a parent. It took her a while to understand that he simply wanted to bond with the male figure in his life.

"I miss you, though," Ryan said.

"I miss you, too, honey. You always have a home here whenever you want."

"I know. But right now I love it here. I don't see myself ever wanting to leave this place."

Ever?

Mackenzie couldn't help but feel a pang of sadness at his words. "So what's so great about L.A. anyway?" As if she didn't know what he'd say.

"Do you even have to ask?" He chuckled. "It's Hollywood, Mom, where things are happening."

She could only imagine. "Things that maybe are way too mature for a fifteen-year-old."

"Not those types of things," he clarified. "I mean like fun, adventure, seeing celebrities walking around like normal people, having the beach at practically walking distance, stuff like that."

"I suppose there are lots of pretty girls out there, too?" Mackenzie couldn't help but ask, knowing he was at an age where girls took on greater meaning.

Ryan giggled. "Yeah, too many to count of all colors, shapes, and sizes."

"Sounds more like clothes or cars," she said, laughing.

"There's plenty of cool clothes and cars, too," he noted.

"I'll bet. Try not to take it all in too fast." She didn't want him to lose his perspective out there.

"I won't. Right now I'm just chilling and glad to be where I belong."

In Mackenzie's heart he would always belong in Cheri Village. But she understood he wanted more than the town or she could give him at this time in his life and had to respect that. Didn't make it any easier not being able to see him each and every day.

"Maybe I'll come out for a visit sometime."

"You really want to?" he asked skeptically.

"Of course."

"Won't that be kind of weird, you and Dad, like, breathing the same air?"

Mackenzie gulped, hating him to think they were at war, even if it once seemed that way. "Just because your father and I are no longer together doesn't mean we can't be civilized. Besides, I would think that the smog there would present far more problems with breathing the air."

Ryan laughed. "Good point."

"What's important is that the two of you are able to communicate." After all, that was the hope in letting him go live with his father.

"Yeah, we're talking."

"That's great." Mackenzie paused. "And things are still well with your stepmother?"

"She hasn't kicked me out of the house yet," he quipped. "So I guess we're able to live under the same roof."

"The adjustment works both ways, Ryan."

"I know." He sniffed. "So when are you coming?"

"Probably not till next year. Unless you'd like me to come sooner?" *Say yes,* she hoped. "I'd love to see Disneyland and maybe Beverly Hills."

"Next year is cool," he said. "We can check out those places."

"Good." She bit back disappointment. "I'd better let you get back to what you were doing. Love you."

"Love you, too."

Mackenzie listened thoughtfully as the line went dead.

On Saturday after working on people's hair, Mackenzie spent over an hour in the backyard tending to her flower garden. She'd had a green thumb all her life, helping her mother plant flowers and vegetables at an early age. It gave Mackenzie great joy to watch the fruits of her labor sprout into something lovely. This year she grew pincushion flowers, Lenten rose, purple coneflower and "Endless Summer" hydrangea. She was thinking about adding some day lilies and dahlias to her collection.

Mackenzie heard the sound of a ball pounding concrete. She looked toward Ian's backyard and saw him bouncing a basketball while his dog lunged for it.

"Good afternoon," she said when it was apparent that Ian was peering at her.

"Hey there, neighbor." He tossed the ball toward the grass and Otis chased it. "Nice seeing you again."

"Same here." Mackenzie found it hard to say otherwise. Since their first meeting, he'd made himself scarce. Or was it the other way around? She supposed they both had busy lives, giving them little time to socialize.

Ian moved closer to the fence separating their property. He wore a T-shirt, shorts and athletic shoes. The outfit showed off his rippling muscles.

Mackenzie couldn't help but be impressed.

"So you're a gardener?" he asked as he flashed an intrigued smile.

She looked at her dirt-stained gloves, feeling slightly self-conscious. "That's me, Ms. All-American Gardener."

"Wonderful. I love checking out gardens. Looks like you've put a lot of work into yours."

"If I don't do it, no one else will," she told him candidly.

"Makes sense." He half grinned. "Maybe someday you can help me create a garden back here."

Mackenzie gazed at his dog wrestling with the basketball. She hated to think what he would do to a garden.

"I'm not sure Otis would welcome such company."

Ian chuckled. "You don't know Otis very well yet. Like me, he always welcomes the company of a beautiful woman."

I walked right into that one. Though she didn't feel very beautiful at the moment, Mackenzie had to hand it to him for being charming. Not to mention very easy on the eyes.

"We'll see about that."

"Anytime."

The dog rolled over and nudged the ball back toward Ian and he picked it up.

He faced the basketball hoop he had put up, dribbled once and took a jump shot, hitting nothing but the net. Three more such shots followed with the same result.

Mackenzie pretended not to notice that he was obviously showing off his court skills. She wondered what other things he excelled in.

Do I really want to know?

Mackenzie had barely gone back to her gardening when she heard him ask, "You play?"

She looked up. Ian was gazing directly at her as he held the ball just out of reach of his dog.

"A little." In fact, she was a starting guard on her high-school team back in the day. But saw no reason to tip her hand at this point.

"Want to come over and shoot with me?"

Mackenzie had pretty much wrapped up her garden work for the day and was ready for a shower. So maybe that could wait for half an hour while she showed her handsome neighbor a few moves.

"Sure, why not?"

Ian was surprised when Mackenzie took him up on his offer to play ball. Most women would have been too concerned about breaking a nail or messing up their hair. Clearly Mackenzie was not only gorgeous, but athletic, a quality he admired in a woman.

He tossed the ball her way when she came into the backyard, knowing that Otis would want to size Mackenzie up. Frankly, so did he.

If the lady was unnerved, she didn't show it. Ian watched her handle Otis's playfulness with ease and then take a shot, banking it off the backboard and into the net.

"Very good," he said, impressed with her skill and even more so with her body language. Even in her stained, baggy clothing, she looked sexy as hell. "Or was that just beginner's luck?"

Mackenzie batted her eyes. "I don't think so." She grabbed the ball and calmly sank another.

He cracked a smile. "All skill, I stand corrected."

"Care to play a game of HORSE?" She tossed the ball at him. "Or are you afraid to get shown up in front of your dog?"

Ian laughed. The lady had spunk, as well as other assets. "You're on."

He handed her the ball so she could go first. Not his best move, as she quickly took the lead.

"Where did you learn to shoot?" he asked.

"High school," she admitted. "I was on the team for two years."

He feigned disappointment. "Figures I end up living next to a basketball star."

Mackenzie smiled. "Maybe once upon a time. Right now, I'm just a thirty-something neighbor who can whip your butt on the court."

Ian flashed his teeth at her. "You just keep thinking that and we'll see who ends up winning."

"Yes, we will." She hit another shot and even Otis seemed in awe.

Ian picked up the ball on a bounce and tried a jump hook. He missed.

Mackenzie tracked down the ball and eyed him. "So do you live in that great big house all by yourself?"

Is she asking purely out of curiosity or because she's interested? he wondered.

"Not exactly." He glanced at Otis. "I've got my best friend to keep me company." But he was open to some attractive female companionship.

"I see."

He wasn't sure she did, so Ian decided to make it perfectly clear. "I'm single. How about you?"

Mackenzie licked her lips. "Same here. Actually I'm divorced."

Ian's brow lifted. It wasn't that he was surprised she was

divorced, since he was well aware of divorce statistics these days. His real shock was that some guy got a lady like her to walk down the aisle, only to end up losing her.

Not that he was one to talk, given that he'd never been engaged, much less married. But that didn't mean he was dumb enough to let someone who had captured his heart and soul get away, should such a woman ever come into his life.

"What do you do for a living, if you don't mind my asking?" Mackenzie tilted her head. "Or are you independently wealthy?"

"I wish." Ian never believed for one moment that she was looking for a sugar daddy. "I'm in communications. You?" He assumed she wasn't living off a rich uncle or something.

"I co-own a hair salon."

Ian could imagine that. "Now I'll know where to go when I need my head shaved."

She cracked a smile. "Our doors are always open to new customers."

"Great." He wondered if the door was open to a neighbor who was in the market for some hot passion with the right woman. Hard to believe this beauty could be all by her lonesome in the dating department.

"H-O-R…" Mackenzie called out.

"Don't get too comfortable," he warned, refocusing on the game. "That S-E will never happen."

They traded shots and Ian's naturally competitive instincts told him to go all out for victory. But the side of him that was smitten with Mackenzie saw no real benefit in edging her out in the game.

And so when he had the chance to do just that, Ian purposely made his shot go slightly wide, bouncing off the rim.

"I win!" Mackenzie laughed and gave him a high-five.

"Yeah, you got me," he told her.

"Maybe next time you'll let me be when I'm tending to my garden."

So there will be a next time? He was all for that and possibly with a different result.

Ian tossed the ball for Otis to chase. "Win some, lose some. I'm man enough to take one on the chin without falling to pieces."

"That's good to know. Not all men are."

"Or women," he reminded her.

"True enough."

"I don't know about you, but I've built up quite a thirst." Ian gazed down at her. "Would you like to come in? I'll get us some lemonade, beer, wine…you name it."

She seemed to mull it over. "Thanks for the invitation, but I'm kind of dirty and sweaty. I'll take a rain check, though."

"You've got it." He didn't mention how much the idea of getting dirty and sweaty with her turned him on. Maybe one of these days they would get to work up a sweat a different way.

"Enjoy your basketball," Mackenzie told him before walking out of the yard, leaving Ian wanting so much more.

Chapter 3

Mackenzie was surprised to find Sophia approaching just as she was leaving Ian's backyard.

"What are you doing here?" Mackenzie asked, though she had a pretty good idea.

"Oh, I just happened to be in the neighborhood and…"

"You're such a snoop. You came by on the chance of meeting my neighbor."

"Something like that." Sophia grinned unabashedly. "I heard the two of you playing in the backyard."

Mackenzie shrugged. "No big deal."

"Says who?" Sophia looked over her shoulder. "Hi, you must be the new neighbor?"

Mackenzie turned to see Ian walk up, Otis at his side wagging his tail.

"That I am," he said. "And you are?"

"Sophia Rockford. I'm Mackenzie's partner and best friend."

"Nice to meet you." He lifted his hand and they shook.

"You, too."

Sophia beamed and Mackenzie felt that they'd held hands just a little too long for her comfort. On top of that, she now felt self-conscious in her dirty, sweaty garden clothes while Sophia was dressed to kill as usual in a double-breasted pantsuit.

"And who might this be?" Sophia bent down to pet the dog.

"Otis."

"Hi, Otis. I think Labs are very intriguing animals."

Ian faced her with interest. "Really?"

Mackenzie recalled Sophia telling her that she needed to get to know more about the dog to know the man.

Maybe she's trying to beat me to the punch.

She grabbed Sophia's hand. "We're leaving now, Ian. I'm sure you have better things to do with your time than gab with us."

He tossed his head back with laughter. "I'm sure I can think of something. Whenever you want a rematch, let me know."

"I'll do that." Mackenzie chalked that up to another victory of sorts.

"Bye, Sophia," he said.

"Bye-bye." She waved as she was led by Mackenzie back to her house.

Inside, Mackenzie confronted her. "What the hell was that about?"

Sophia batted her fake eyelashes. "I'm sure I don't know what you mean."

"You know exactly what I mean," Mackenzie said. "You were shamelessly coming on to Ian."

"I was not!"

"That's not the way I saw it."

"Oh, don't get so bent out of shape for nothing," said Sophia, putting an arm around her. "I was just being friendly to your new neighbor, that's all."

Mackenzie wrinkled her nose. Perhaps she'd overreacted. But that didn't change the fact that rail-thin, natural flirts like Sophia tended to attract men.

Was Ian attracted to Sophia?

"Anyway," Sophia shrugged, "he's not really my type."

"I thought every good-looking man was your type," Mackenzie teased her.

"Not the ones who obviously have their eye on someone else."

"You mean me?"

"Who else?"

Mackenzie was glad to hear that, but still tried to downplay it. "All we did was play basketball. That hardly means the man is interested."

Sophia looked at her. "Don't fool yourself. Next to cozying up to a man's pet, playing sports with him is the best way to spark a man's interest."

Mackenzie conceded that there did seem to be chemistry between them and an easy, flowing rapport. But she wasn't looking too far ahead just yet.

She scanned her friend. "So why is it I never see you on the court and dressed for the part?"

Sophia tossed her Senegalese twists. "Because I rely on other effective means to get a man."

"Such as?"

"Appealing to his sense of style and appreciation for the finer things a woman can offer."

Mackenzie studied her fingernail. "I think I bring that to the table, too."

"Of course you do," Sophia agreed. "All I'm saying is there's more than one way to get a man. The more ways you use, the better your chances for success."

Mackenzie contemplated her words. She was happy to get

to know her neighbor. Only time would tell if her qualities as
a lady and experience as a woman would lead to something
more with Ian.

Ian took a shower after shooting hoops with Mackenzie.
He loved the way her nicely rounded bottom moved from side
to side and up and down as she dribbled, set up to shoot and
released the ball. She definitely had good form and the type
of body that left him drooling. He hoped they got together for
more athletic events.

Even beyond that, Mackenzie captured his fancy. Even
when she was dressing down she was able to work magic on
his libido like few women ever could. That made him want
to delve deeper into their connection and let it play out for all
they could achieve together, sexually and otherwise.

Could be Mackenzie had just what he was looking for in a
woman, beauty aside. And he'd be a damn fool not to pursue her.

Apparently the feeling was mutual. He'd seen Mackenzie
give Sophia a green-eyed look when it appeared that she was
coming on to him. He liked that Mackenzie was already
getting territorial before they had even forged a partnership
worth fighting for. It told him she, too, wanted to see where
this was going without competition getting in the way.

As it was, Ian was not interested in dating Sophia. She was
an attractive lady for sure and obviously knew how to play up
her assets. But he'd been down that road before. Women who
looked like they had just stepped off the runway were fun eye
candy, but he was looking for something more.

These days, he was looking for someone who was in great
shape without being skin and bones. He wanted a woman
who attracted him sexually, but also had a nice sense of humor
and challenged him with her personality. Mackenzie seemed
to hit the mark on all counts. Ian looked forward to getting to

know her much better. He also hoped to show her more of who he was as a man and a lover, should things heat up to that degree. At this stage it was just a matter of time until he and Mackenzie got together. The question was—would it be his place or hers?

Chapter 4

Two days later Mackenzie was working out at the gym with her friend Estelle Joplin. The two had met at a party when they were both married. They hadn't been as close since Mackenzie's divorce, but they still got together every now and then. Estelle was also one of the salon's clients.

Mackenzie tried her best to listen to Estelle talk about her husband, Talbot, and how he'd put in extra effort to spice up their love life, but her mind kept drifting back to Ian. She couldn't believe she'd taken such a bold move in cozying up to him in his backyard. The last thing Mackenzie wanted was for the man to think she was desperate. Especially since she still couldn't be sure if he really was available, or just playing the field. But the way he'd been scoping her out told Mackenzie that Ian was at least as interested in her as she was him.

"So what do you think?" Estelle put a snap in her voice to

get Mackenzie's attention as they rode side by side on elliptical machines.

Mackenzie fluttered her lashes. "I'm sorry. I was thinking about work. What was that last part?"

"I said that Talbot wants to spend our anniversary in the Bahamas."

"What do *you* want?" Mackenzie asked, fully rejoining the conversation.

Estelle took a deep breath. "Well I've been there and done that. I was thinking Hawaii might be nice. I've always wanted to visit Maui."

"Then that's your answer," Mackenzie told her. "Hawaii, here you come. Talbot only wants to make you happy."

"Yeah, he knows a good thing when he has it." Estelle moved a little faster as if to demonstrate the shapeliness of her curves. "Too bad Brent wasn't so smart."

Mackenzie agreed but refused to harp on it. "That's not the way Brent saw it. As far as he was concerned, sleeping with and marrying his secretary was the smartest move he could have made."

"It'll never last. Ditching you for some sex kitten half his age is something he'll regret," Estelle tried to reassure Mackenzie.

"Actually, it was me who ditched him." Mackenzie set the record straight for the umpteenth time. "Brent was perfectly willing to have his cake and frosting, too. But I wasn't going to stand for it."

"You did the right thing," Estelle said.

That was a change of heart, as she had previously insisted for the sake of the family, that Mackenzie give Brent a second chance. The problem was it hadn't been the first time Brent cheated on her and it certainly wouldn't have been the last. Mackenzie had finally reached the breaking point in the relationship and did what was best for her and

Ryan. Neither of them needed a part-time husband and father.

The fact that Ryan now chose to live with his father concerned Mackenzie in this regard. She didn't want her son to think it was perfectly acceptable to treat a woman the way Brent had treated her. But she believed that as a successful businessman and college graduate who loved his son, Brent's presence would be invaluable to Ryan. Mackenzie could only hope that was enough to make their relationship work while Ryan adjusted to life with his stepmother.

Estelle wiped perspiration from her brow. "If you ask me, Brent will come running back. Most men do when they realize the grass on the other side is more brown than green."

Mackenzie sneered. "Excuse me, but I don't want Brent back. The last thing I need is to be with a man I can't trust."

"People can change, you know."

Mackenzie would never go down that road again. Not when there were other men out there who had so much to offer a woman *and* give her the respect she deserved.

"Some marriages are simply not meant to be," she told Estelle. "Present company excluded, of course. But I think I'll take my chances in the open market, thank you."

Her friend's coffee-brown eyes widened. "Are you saying you've met someone?"

Mackenzie debated whether to tell Estelle about Ian. Maybe she was jumping the gun. After all, nothing had happened between her and the sexy neighbor…yet.

"Not anyone I'm ready to tie the knot with," she responded evasively. "You just never know who might be waiting around the corner." Or next door.

Mackenzie felt her muscles aching, but kept her arms and legs moving. Yes, she was in great shape, but that didn't mean there wasn't room for improvement. Especially when she had someone new to impress.

Ian took advantage of the open spaces at the park to go for a run. Otis accompanied him and seemed tireless, giving Ian someone to keep up with rather than the other way around. He held on to the dog's leash tightly, not wanting Otis to break loose and get into trouble.

Having been a runner since college, Ian felt it was the purest form of exercise since it worked every part of the body. He wondered if Mackenzie also ran, which would only add another plus to go along with her basketball and gardening skills.

The mere thought of Mackenzie seemed to make Ian's heart beat faster. But Ian began his cool down, much to Otis's chagrin, as the dog clearly preferred to continue running.

"There will be plenty of other times for you to do your thing, boy," Ian told him.

Indeed, Ian believed there would be ample time for both of them to get acclimated to their surroundings.

Which included cozying up to a friendly neighbor.

Upon getting within reach of his house, Ian released Otis from the leash, expecting him to run up to the porch. Instead, the dog spotted a squirrel and took off after it. Both headed right toward Mackenzie's backyard.

"Stop, Otis!" Ian's voice boomed, but the dog paid no attention. Ian prayed Mackenzie's back gate was closed. The barrier would pose no problem for the squirrel, but it would stop Otis in his tracks.

When Ian arrived at the house he saw that Mackenzie's gate was open, though her car was gone. Otis disappeared into her yard.

Damn. "Otis, get out of there right now!"

Ian got a sinking feeling as he approached the yard. He was afraid that Otis had really gone to town on Mackenzie's garden. The lady would surely be pissed, and that was definitely not a good way to start off their budding friendship.

Otis came running out of the yard as if his tail had caught fire. Ian grabbed him, quickly attaching the leash.

"Bad boy! What happened to the squirrel?" There was no indication Otis had caught the squirrel, which was a good sign. "I hope you left her yard the same way you found it."

Ian went back to have a look. He saw clear evidence that some plants had been damaged, but it was far from a total disaster. Now all he had to do was convince Mackenzie of that. And he had the perfect opportunity as Mackenzie's car began to make its way up the driveway.

Mackenzie was surprised to find Ian and his dog standing in front of her house. But that was only half as surprising as seeing the open gate to her backyard. Before she jumped to any conclusions she wanted to hear Ian's explanation.

She exited the car and Ian greeted her with a big smile.

"How are you today?" he asked tentatively, holding the dog's leash tightly.

"Fine." Mackenzie met Ian's gaze. "So what's going on?"

"Not much, really."

"Why is my gate open?"

"You must have left it open," he said flatly.

Her eyes rolled disbelievingly. "Did your dog do something to my yard?"

Ian hesitated. "Well, he chased a squirrel and kind of got into your flower garden a little."

"Yeah, right." She stormed past Otis and his owner to survey the damage.

At first Mackenzie saw nothing to cause concern, until her

gaze landed on what looked like a half-chewed and half-stampeded hydrangea.

She turned to face Ian, who had been following her. "You let your dog come into my yard and ruin my flowers?"

Ian cocked a brow. "As I said, he got loose and tried to catch a squirrel."

"And that's supposed to justify this?" Mackenzie snapped.

"Maybe if you'd kept your gate closed—"

"Whoa, just hold up a minute." Her nostrils flared. "Now you're blaming *me* for what *your* dog did?"

Ian gave a tiny chuckle. "Not at all. I take full responsibility for that."

"It's not funny," she told him, getting the feeling that he didn't take this seriously or respect the work that went into maintaining a garden.

Ian sighed. "Of course not. I never suggested such."

"Yeah, right. I would expect you to dismiss it as amusing."

"That's not the case," he said as Otis simply stared at her unapologetically.

Mackenzie sneered. "My garden is not a place for your dog to play around with squirrels or any other creatures"

"I wouldn't exactly call it playing," Ian told her. "It's a dog's nature to go after smaller creatures. Otis just happened to latch onto the wrong one at the wrong time."

"I'm not interested in your philosophizing about this," she spoke bluntly. "It should never have happened and I lay the fault entirely on you."

Ian bristled. "I can't argue against that. It's also not the end of the world. I mean, with all due respect, they're *just* flowers and can easily be replaced."

Mackenzie's eyes became slits, though she wasn't at all surprised that he would be so cavalier about this. "That's hardly the point. Flowers do not bloom overnight. Nor do they plant themselves. I'm also a busy woman and do not have the time to clean up the mess your dog made."

"So I'll do it," he said testily.

"Oh, no." She shook her head adamantly. "The last thing I need is for you to make things worse."

Ian frowned. "Doesn't look like I can win for losing here. I apologized for what Otis did. I'll pay for the cost to replace the damned flowers and your labor. Just send me a bill."

Mackenzie's eyes widened. "I don't want your money."

"Then what? My head on a platter? Or maybe Otis's?"

Mackenzie took a breath, not wanting to lose it altogether. She glanced at the dog, who seemed as sweet and innocent as could be. Except when it came to chasing squirrels. And stomping her flowers.

"All I ask is that you keep your dog out of my yard from now on."

"No problem," Ian said succinctly.

"Good."

Ian tugged at the dog's leash. "C'mon, boy, let's get you back home before you cause another mess."

Mackenzie felt there was more that should be said, but she wasn't sure what. She watched Ian and Otis walk away while wondering if she'd reacted too harshly.

She looked at the gate. Had she really forgotten to close it this morning?

If so, that would make her at least partially responsible for what had happened. After all, that was why she'd gotten a gate in the first place—to keep animals, stray or otherwise, from getting into her garden. Turning back toward the ruined flowers, Mackenzie now knew what was on her agenda this weekend.

No thanks to Ian and Otis.

Chapter 5

"You did what?" Sophia's eyes bulged.

Mackenzie sucked in a deep breath. She knew she should have kept this to herself.

Sophia paused to look at Mackenzie. She was in the middle of trimming a client's hair.

Mackenzie repeated herself. "I told Ian that his dog isn't welcome in my yard."

"Isn't that counterproductive to getting to know the man better?" Sophia asked.

Mackenzie had considered that very thought a number of times. She was still attracted to Ian. How could she not be? But that didn't mean his dog could take liberties in her garden.

"He obviously didn't have Otis on a leash when he went after a squirrel. Do you know how long I worked on those 'Endless Summer' hydrangeas?"

"I think you've told me often enough. But maybe you work

on your garden too much and don't spend enough time working on your social life."

Mackenzie heard her client laugh, making her do the same,
though self-consciously. She didn't exactly want to announce
to the whole world that she was single and had ended up
making bad choices when it came to men. She wondered if
she had been overcompensating for that by devoting hours to
trying to make her garden the best it could be.

"I like gardening," she responded stubbornly. "And any
man who likes me has to respect that—including his dog."

"I agree." Sophia rinsed the woman's hair. "All I'm saying
is you need to cut the man some slack. Dogs will be dogs.
Maybe you should have Ian come over and help you plant new
hydrangeas. That might clear the air."

"I'm pretty sure he's not the gardening type."

"And what makes you think that?"

Mackenzie swallowed. "The gardening type who would
never let their dog trample a garden," she answered
thoughtfully.

After work Mackenzie went to the computer and looked
up Labrador retrievers. She figured at the very least she should
get to know a little something about the dog and what made
Otis tick besides his owner. Right away she learned that Labs
were fiercely loyal, good with children, loved to eat and fun-
oriented. She suspected that last part was where the squirrel-
chasing came in.

Recalling Sophia's advice about getting to know a man's
dog, Mackenzie read about the history of Labradors, famous
ones, and their characteristics. She could see now why Ian had
picked a Lab for a pet. Or maybe it was the other way around?

Mackenzie regretted the heated exchange with Ian. She
had gone over the top in her reaction. Otis really hadn't
done that much damage to her garden. She hoped the

incident didn't derail the more than neighborly vibes between her and Ian. But someone had to make the first move.

Three days had passed since Ian had spoken to Mackenzie, though she was always on his mind. He was pretty sure she was still upset that Otis had gotten into her flower garden. He probably should have handled the situation differently, as he had no doubt come across as cavalier.

But what was done was done. He couldn't go back in time and keep Otis on the leash and out of Mackenzie's garden. What Ian could do was try to make amends. Mackenzie was a lady worth getting to know better. Aside from the sexuality that radiated from every part of her body and the good form she showed playing basketball, there was something about Mackenzie that drew him to her. Ian couldn't recall ever being this strongly attracted to another woman. He didn't want to waste the chemistry between them. Besides, staying on good terms with his closest neighbor seemed the smart thing to do.

With a bottle of Sangiovese in hand, Ian knocked on Mackenzie's door. He hoped she liked wine.

More importantly, I hope she likes me enough to let bygones be bygones.

The door opened and he saw Mackenzie standing there barefoot, looking sexier than a woman had a right to be.

"Hi," he said.

"Hello." She regarded him up and down and seemed to approve his attire of a striped shirt, dark stonewashed jeans and loafers.

"Brought over a peace offering."

"Did you now?" Mackenzie flashed a grin.

"Yeah." He lifted the bottle.

She took the wine and studied it. "Good choice."

"It's one of my favorites," Ian replied, surprised to see Mackenzie smiling.

"Would you like a glass?" Mackenzie offered.

"I'd love one."

Mackenzie smiled. "Come in."

Ian walked past her and got a whiff of a fresh scent as if she'd just taken a bath. Immediately Ian was taken in by the ambiance. He followed her into the kitchen. Mackenzie took out two glasses and set them down before opening the bottle.

"Nice place you've got here," Ian told her.

"Thanks." She handed him a filled glass. "How's Otis?"

He grinned uneasily. "He's fine. Just sleeping right now."

"I didn't think he ever took a break," Mackenzie said playfully.

"Yeah, seems that way sometimes." He took a sip of wine. "Look, about the other day—"

She cut him off. "It's over. Let's just move on."

"Sounds good to me." Ian breathed a sigh of relief that they would be able to get past his poor judgment in releasing Otis from his leash at precisely the wrong moment. Especially when he wanted nothing more than to get closer to his neighbor. Even now she was turning him on like crazy.

"Would you like to sit down?" Mackenzie asked graciously.

"Sure, as long as I'm not keeping you from anything."

"Not at all. I'd love to have some company."

A tiny smile emerged on Ian's lips.

They sat at the hardwood dining table. Ian noted a baker's rack in the corner alongside a potted plant. Next to that was a framed photograph on the top shelf of Mackenzie and a teenage boy.

"That's my son, Ryan," Mackenzie said as she saw Ian's gaze focus on the picture. "He lives with his father in California."

"Oh."

Ian hadn't seen that coming. He probably shouldn't have made the assumption that she was childless. Many women in their mid-thirties stood a good chance of being mothers.

Mackenzie looked directly at Ian. "Do you have any kids?"

"No."

"You never wanted any?"

Ian felt as though he'd been put on the spot. He didn't want to say the wrong thing. "Let's just say that I'm not really the daddy type."

Her eyes narrowed. "And what type is that?"

He paused, shrugging. "The diaper-changing type, I guess."

Mackenzie laughed.

"Yeah." Ian lifted the glass. "That's not to say I wouldn't own up to my part as a parent if I were to become a father."

"You mean by accident?"

"That, or if I were with someone I really cared for who wanted a child." Or already had one, though he preferred not to have to deal with the drama often associated with children.

Ian sipped the wine, all the while thinking that Mackenzie was the type of woman who could make him rethink his position.

"So you're from Connecticut?"

"Yeah." He thought of the license plate. "Have you been there?"

"No, but I've always wanted to see the Maritime Aquarium and the historic homes in Wethersfield."

Ian was impressed with the range of her interests. "I've been to Wethersfield a couple of times. It is amazing there and I'm sure you'd enjoy it." Just as he was enjoying her company now.

"I'd love to," Mackenzie said. "If only I had more time."

"Maybe you should make the time. It's not that far from here. I'd even volunteer to be your tour guide."

"Really?" Her lashes fluttered.

"Sure, why not?" Ian imagined that he could get used to doing anything with her.

"Well, I'll keep that in mind. Would you like some more wine?"

"Only if you'll join me in another glass."

She smiled in agreement.

Loving to see the sweet curve of her lips and tiny dimples in her cheeks, Ian watched Mackenzie as she got up and refilled their glasses. He could only imagine what it would be like to see her body free of clothing, his hands exploring every inch of her flesh.

Ian quickly erased the thought from his mind only because he didn't want to get too aroused. But if things continued to progress between them, he just might get to see his fantasy turn into reality.

"I knew the people who lived in the house before you," Mackenzie said, handing him the refilled glass.

"How were they?"

"Good people."

"Why did they move?" Ian was only mildly curious.

"A job transfer took them abroad."

He wondered if she regretted their move. Or was she as tuned into present company as he was?

"I'd like to thank them for giving me the opportunity to move into a beautiful home with a gorgeous neighbor."

Mackenzie blushed. "Oh stop. You're too much."

"You think? I'm just stating the truth."

"Well, since we're getting personal here, I think you're very handsome, too."

Ian grinned. "Blame it on my father."

"Your mother doesn't share any of the responsibility?"

"She does. But I got most of my physical characteristics from him, so I guess he had the stronger genes."

"I see."

Ian studied her. "Who do you favor more—your mother or father?"

Mackenzie tapped her chin as if thinking about it deeply. "I'd have to say both of them."

"Why am I not surprised?"

"Hey, I can't help it if they were equal contributors in the gene pool." She laughed and he followed suit.

Ian decided now seemed like a great time to go for it. "You want to go out sometime?"

Mackenzie's eyes widened. "As in a *date?*"

"Yeah, or two friendly neighbors hanging out, if that works better for you."

"I think I like the date better."

"So do I." Ian flashed his teeth. He glanced at his watch, not wanting to press his luck. "Well, I'm sure Otis is awake and ready for some chow."

"Then you'd better go feed him," Mackenzie said as she stood.

Ian stood up along with her and Mackenzie walked him to the door.

"Thanks for the wine."

"My pleasure." He zeroed in on her luscious mouth, wanting to kiss her tantalizing lips more than anything.

But he also wanted to show some restraint.

"See you later," he said, and then went out the door.

Mackenzie was sure Ian was going to kiss her. Instead his eyes turned away, leaving her slightly disappointed. She said goodbye and closed the door.

Maybe it was the wine that had her wanting the man in a way she hadn't wanted any other for so long. She wondered if he felt the same. Mackenzie thought back to their conver-

sation about children. She had a son and Ian was childless
with little desire to change that. She wondered if that would
prove to be an issue in whatever future possibilities might
develop between them. She hoped not. Ian seemed like the
kind of man with whom she could see sparks turning into
flames. A fire that might not be so easy to extinguish.

Mackenzie allowed her imagination to roam further. She
could literally feel Ian's hands all over her and their mouths
connected in a mouthwatering kiss before making love the
entire night through. And when the morning sun arrived they
were thoroughly exhausted and fell asleep in each other's
arms. Neither had any desire to separate anytime soon....

Mackenzie snapped out of the erotic reverie. Her nipples
were tingling and armpits were wet. She couldn't believe
she'd just enacted in her head a steamy sex scene with Ian.
She felt embarrassed by it and encouraged at the same time
that her womanhood was still intact. Clearly the absence of a
significant other in her life had begun to have an effect.
Romantic men with an eye on her didn't come along every
day. Certainly one the likes of Ian Kelly.

Again Mackenzie thought about the kiss that had never
occurred and could have proven to be quite interesting. She
considered going over to his place and initiating contact
between their lips. How would Ian react? Would one step lead
to another, then another till there was no stopping them...?

Though the notion excited her, Mackenzie rejected such a
bold move. Being a conservative gal in many respects, she still
believed it was better that the man at least make the first
move. Then they could go from there. She had a feeling it was
only a matter of time before mutual sexual attraction would
lead to more from Ian than a bottle of wine and friendly conversation between neighbors.

Wanting to take her mind off Ian, Mackenzie decided to

go shopping, something she didn't do enough of these days between her other obligations. When she returned home, she saw Ian and Otis sitting on their porch. Her heart missed a beat, and she realized it was because of the sex fantasy she'd had earlier.

Just be calm and he'll never suspect a thing.

She got out of her car with two bags. "Hey," she said, smiling.

"Looks like someone's been spending money," Ian said.

"Not that much."

"Why don't you put that inside and come join us for a bit? Otis wants to apologize his own way for getting into your garden."

Mackenzie laughed. "You mean by biting me?"

"He'd never do that—not to someone he actually likes."

And just how much does his owner like me? Mackenzie felt this might be a good time to impress Ian about her newfound knowledge of Labrador retrievers. Bonding with Otis couldn't hurt matters any either, as Mackenzie wanted to get closer to Ian any way she could.

"Give me five minutes," she told him.

Ian was glad he'd been on the porch when Mackenzie returned home. Ever since leaving her house earlier he had been able to think of practically nothing other than what it would feel like to kiss her. He suspected the feeling was mutual. But he still didn't want to jump the gun and get carried away with the aches of his libido. If they were on the verge of a relationship, he preferred that it move on a pace that put no undue pressure on either of them. When the time was right, he fully expected them to move to the next level.

Mackenzie seemed tuned into Otis at the moment, making it clear that there were no hard feelings. She petted him and rubbed his head. Otis ate it up, licking her fingers and whimpering like a lovesick puppy.

"Looks like you two have become best buds," Ian said, grinning.

Mackenzie, who was on her knees, smiled up at him. "Let's just say we are a work in progress."

"You're progressing pretty well, I'd say."

"Labs are easy to like once you get past squirrel-chasing and focus on how cute they are."

Ian lifted a brow. "Cute, huh?"

"Yes," Mackenzie said. "And smart, too. Did you know that Labradors are very intelligent?"

"Are they, now?" Ian regarded her with amusement. "Didn't know my dog had some Einstein in him."

"Maybe you don't know Otis as well as you think," she told him, getting to her feet. "Labs have a lot of initiative and understanding. They're great as guide dogs, for hunting, detection and therapy."

Ian chuckled. "Looks like you've done your homework."

"Something like that." Mackenzie licked her lips. "Seemed like before I condemned Otis, I should at least get to know the breed."

"I couldn't agree more." Ian got to his feet. He was moved that she had taken the time to really get acquainted with his dog. "I'm sure Otis appreciates it. And so do I."

She batted her eyes teasingly. "Seemed the neighborly thing to do."

He gazed at her mouth, ripe and ready to be kissed. "So is this…"

Ian cupped Mackenzie's cheeks and tilted her face, bringing her forward for a kiss. Her lips were soft and sweet, as he imagined her body to be. It was a sensual step in the right direction and one he was content to enjoy to the fullest.

Chapter 6

The following day, Mackenzie smiled at Ryan's handsome face on the computer screen. They were having a video conversation. She still found it hard to believe sometimes that Internet technology allowed two people the ability to see and speak to each other from anywhere in the world.

Ryan looked like his father, with the same refined features and closely cropped dark hair. She couldn't help but think about Ian, who had said he favored his own father. Only Ian had no interest in passing the same physical traits to progeny of his own. Mackenzie couldn't fault him for that. Not everyone embraced having a family.

"I can see that you've been spending a lot of time in the sun," she told Ryan, noting that he appeared happy and healthy.

"Yep." He gave a crooked grin. "I like being outside. There's always something to do here."

"As long as you don't get into any trouble." She considered the hazards of adolescence—drugs, gangs and teen sex. Though Ryan had never been a bad kid, Mackenzie wasn't there now to help keep him on the straight and narrow. It was up to her ex to make sure Ryan stayed in line.

He wrinkled his nose. "You don't have to worry about me."

"It's called being a mother," she said unapologetically.

"I know. I hang out with some pretty cool friends. No one wants to do anything crazy."

"That's good to hear." She knew he would be returning to school next month. "Just make sure when school starts you keep your grades up so you can get into college."

"I plan to. Dad knows someone in the recruiting office at UCLA. Maybe I'll go there."

"That would be an excellent choice," Mackenzie agreed. She could also think of some fine schools in the Northeast should he choose to get his education closer to home someday.

"Dad and Deborah fight a lot," Ryan said out of the blue.

Mackenzie cocked a brow. This was news to her. Not that Brent ever shared much with her these days. That was fine by her, except where it affected their son.

"What do they fight about?" she asked.

"What don't they fight about?" he responded dryly.

"I thought they got along well?" Or so Brent had led her to believe. What else was he keeping from her?

Ryan snorted. "Think again."

Mackenzie wasn't happy with the thought that Ryan was in a stressful environment. Even if it were his choice. "What do your father and Deborah argue about?" she asked again.

He shrugged. "Different things…"

"Can you be more specific?" She had a feeling he was holding back.

"Bills, the house, what time Dad gets home, whatever…"

Mackenzie wondered if Brent had already tired of his

new wife and gone back to cheating ways. Or was it a question of making too little and spending too much in spite of having a good job?

"Anything else they argue about?" Mackenzie pressed.

Ryan paused and looked away. "Me."

Mackenzie's mouth opened speechlessly. "Why would they fight about you?" As if she couldn't guess.

His lips twisted. "Wish I knew."

Her brow furrowed. "Please tell me what's going on, Ryan. Otherwise I'll just be worried that you're somewhere you shouldn't be."

"She has a lot of stupid rules that I don't always follow," he said with a sneer.

"Such as?"

"Don't do this, don't do that. Do this, do that." Ryan took a breath. "Most times it goes in one ear and out the other."

"Not sure that's the smartest thing to do," Mackenzie told him honestly.

"Whatever."

"How is your father responding to this?"

Ryan scratched his chin. "He sides with me most of the time, and she hates that."

Mackenzie's first thought was to rant and rave about Ryan's stepmother overstepping her bounds. But she'd promised Brent not to interfere in the way they raised him as part of the condition of letting Ryan live in California. That didn't mean things had to remain the way they were indefinitely.

Mackenzie sighed. "You'll have to try harder to follow her rules," she advised her son. "Otherwise they may use it as an excuse to send you back here. I'm sure you don't want that, do you?"

He shook his head. "No, I like it here other than that."

"So do what you have to do to stay on her good side," Mackenzie said. "No one said it would be easy moving away from home and starting a new life. If you truly want this to work, you have to be willing to bend at least a little."

"Yeah, you're right," Ryan acquiesced.

"If you want, I'll talk to your father—"

"No way. I don't want him thinking I went behind his back telling you this."

Mackenzie understood that Ryan did not want to come across as a mama's boy. What fifteen-year-old did? She had to respect this even if she was concerned about the situation.

"If you should change your mind—"

"I'll let you know," he said abruptly.

Mackenzie decided to at least give them some time to work this out. As the now ex-wife, she realized she was walking a fine line between wanting to look out for Ryan's best interests and being meddlesome. Hopefully Brent would step up to the plate and not allow his new wife to make life too difficult for Ryan.

"Stay out of it," Sophia said bluntly over lunch the next day.

Mackenzie moved her salad around the plate. "How can I do that?" She'd shared the news of a potential stumbling block in Ryan living with his father.

"Easily. When I was the new wife, the ex put me through hell trying to micromanage our lives and what I should and shouldn't be allowed to do with the kids."

"That was different—"

"It was exactly the same!" Sophia flipped her hair to the side. "She kicked her man to the curb with good reason, but still wanted to try and dictate the terms of how I disciplined her children. All it did was cause friction in the marriage and eventually played a role in ending it. Unless you want Brent back—or Ryan—you need to let them raise him their own way and you need to get on with your life."

Mackenzie chewed on the thought. She definitely did not want to get romantically involved with her ex again. She was too smart to make the same mistake twice. Especially with the man who had betrayed her and for a while had caused her to rethink wanting any involvement ever again with the male species. Instead she got to think about the man next door and how much he was growing on her in very enticing ways. Ian was certainly very attractive. He was also a great kisser, with lips that were firm and fervent.

There was no denying that Mackenzie was enjoying life as a single woman, with no offspring to occupy every moment of her world. Not that she wouldn't welcome Ryan back home with open arms when it came right down to it. How could she not? He was her son and she loved him dearly, even if he was getting of that age when teenagers thought they were grown. She believed Ryan was still relatively happy where he was, but should that ever change they would both have to deal with it.

"All right, I get it," she told Sophia while grabbing a garlic breadstick. "I have to let go."

Her friend smiled. "Now you're getting back to your senses."

Mackenzie frowned. "Didn't say I had to like it."

"Don't expect you to," Sophia said. "No one likes relinquishing that hold on one you gave birth to, and you can't bear to think of his making it out in the big, bad world on his own."

"It's not like that," argued Mackenzie over a cup of coffee. "I simply want this time in Ryan's life to be with as little out-of-the-way stress and strain as possible. Is that so wrong?"

"Of course not. But you can't control that. No one can. Stress is a fact of life, and he has to learn from it on his own. Or in this case with the help of his dad, if not stepmother."

Mackenzie rolled her eyes, but said nothing. All she could do at this point was hope Ryan kept the lines of communication open in keeping her abreast of the situation.

"You may not want to hear this, but whatever his situation, Ryan is not faultless," Sophia said bluntly.

"Meaning…?"

"Meaning your ex's new wife may be a horrible, vindictive stepmom or not. But let's face it, most teenagers these days want no rules at all. They think they should be allowed to stay out all night, party whenever, drink, have sex, you name it."

"Ryan's not like that," Mackenzie said quietly.

Sophia rolled her eyes. "How do you know what he's like now that the boy's been unleashed into a whole new world in California? My point is, at the very least he's probably up for sowing his oats like other teens, even if it means bending the rules. Could be he just doesn't like his stepmother because she's not you."

"You think?" Mackenzie sipped coffee.

"Hey, the stepmother can never measure up to the real mother, even if she allowed her stepchildren to run rings around her. I say give Ryan some space and allow him to become a man through tough love, if necessary, trial and error."

"You've made your point," conceded Mackenzie. The idea that another woman could step into her shoes as Ryan's mother had been a sore spot all along. But she had to get over it, as this was a reality in life these days, with people divorcing and remarrying left and right. She couldn't allow Ryan to get to her. Or feel sorry for his choice to move to Los Angeles.

What was done was done. She had to think about her life now and what it took to make her happy over and beyond her son and his growing pains. The vision that popped into Mackenzie's head was *Ian*.

Sophia seemed to read her mind. "Besides, it seems to me you've got your hands full right now with your sexy next-door neighbor and his dog drama."

"We've moved past that," Mackenzie was happy to report. Otis was now practically her best friend and Ian was all but hooked now that she'd given him a few pointers about his dog.

Sophia dabbed a napkin to her mouth. "All the more reason to focus on what's really important now."

"Oh, really?" Mackenzie eyed her. "And what might that be?"

"Do I have to spell it out?"

"Please do," Mackenzie said, as though she hadn't a clue what was coming next.

Sophia sighed. "We both know you're into the man and I know he has to be into you. The last thing you need is to be looking over the shoulder of your son's stepmother from afar, when instead you could have that hunk next door massaging your shoulders. Or the other way around."

"Who says we haven't already been doing the shoulder thing?" Mackenzie smiled at her teasingly.

Sophia became wide-eyed. "Hmm… You haven't been holding back on your best friend, have you?"

Mackenzie chuckled. She had a mind to exaggerate and really make her envious, but decided that could wait till there was more substance behind the words.

"Actually we've only kissed thus far," she admitted.

"You go, girlfriend!" Sophia flashed her teeth. "Is he a good kisser?"

"Yes! It was only a short kiss but nice." Mackenzie got dreamy. "I have a feeling there will be longer, more passionate ones in the future."

"More power to you. See, that's what I'm talking about. This is your time to put yourself first and go out there and live. Ryan will be fine, even if it sometimes seems he can't possibly be, without you holding his hand." Sophia grinned slyly.

"Clearly there's someone else now in your life who can do all the hand-holding you need."

"Very true," Mackenzie said feelingly as her sex fantasy involving Ian brought a smile to her face.

Chapter 7

On Saturday afternoon, Ian was doing push-ups, planning to reach fifty, when his cell phone rang. He stopped at forty-five and answered.

It was his college buddy Julius Garrison, who happened to live in Burlington.

"You're a hard man to reach," Julius complained.

Ian didn't argue the point. "Yeah, I know. It's been crazy with the move, getting acclimated to the job and so forth."

"I hear you, having gone down that road on more than one occasion myself."

Ian recalled some of those misadventures from back in the day. He wasn't as privy to his old friend's comings and goings in recent memory, as both had branched off in different directions.

"I've been meaning to contact you," Ian insisted, given that he knew few people locally aside from his new colleagues and a couple of neighbors, one in particular who stood out.

"Yeah, I've heard that before," Julius said skeptically. "So I beat you to the punch."

"Guess you did at that." Otis came over, and Ian scratched his head while feeling a trifle guilty. "How's Gwen?"

"That was wife number two." Julius laughed self-consciously. "I'm on number three now—Yasmine."

Ian gave a suppressed chuckle. "My apologies."

"Don't worry about it. Sometimes I have trouble trying to remember who's who myself."

Ian tried to picture himself going down the aisle *three* times. He'd be lucky if it ever happened once. Or maybe it was less about luck and more about just being able to find a woman who was the complete package.

Someone like Mackenzie. Ian was confident that she had the right stuff for any man. He also believed she was ready and willing to share the qualities she possessed with the right man. It just might be him.

"Are you still playing the field?" Julius asked.

"Not really."

"Too bad—there are always hot ladies at the club."

Julius owned a jazz club, which was right up Ian's alley in many respects, given his love for jazz. He loved the mellow, laid-back atmosphere and sultry vocalists who could make standards into their own music. But as far as engaging in nightclub games of pick up and lie down, that wasn't who he was anymore, if ever. These days he was far more interested in substance over temporary appeasement.

"No harm in looking, so long as I don't touch," Ian said largely for effect.

"Whatever you say, man."

Ian touched his chin. "I'm looking forward to checking it out."

"You're welcome anytime."

After disconnecting, Ian went to his computer and checked his stock portfolio. He assessed the gains and losses before heading to the shower. It was there that Mackenzie occupied his thoughts, along with images of kissing her passionately.

Mackenzie drove to the Deer Lounge in Burlington, where she performed every other Saturday as a jazz vocalist. She had been singing since she was in the junior choir—it was in her blood. But during her marriage this talent had been squelched by a husband who had offered no encouragement whatsoever. He had been more attuned to his career and his stereotypical expectations of a wife. It was only after the marriage ended that Mackenzie had decided to pursue her passion.

Julius Garrison, owner of the Deer Lounge, gave her that opportunity. Mackenzie was grateful to be able to use her incredible voice to belt out tunes for the ages before a captive audience. While she had no intention of quitting her day job anytime soon, Mackenzie had found her true calling in music and hoped it would always be a part of her life. She also wanted to find a man who could equally appreciate jazz and her interpretation of it.

Julius greeted Mackenzie when she walked in the door. "The lady of the evening has arrived."

"Hi, Julius," Mackenzie said with a smile.

"And might I say, you are looking as gorgeous as ever."

Mackenzie soaked up the compliment though she hadn't done her makeup or changed into her performance attire yet.

Julius was tall and solid with black-and-blond pixie braids. Though married, he was still a big flirt. He'd been hitting on Mackenzie from the start, but he never crossed the line. She was happy with that. For one thing she never mixed business with pleasure. For another, she didn't fool around with married men. Not even handsome ones.

"You ready to bring the house down with your sultry voice?" Julius followed her toward the dressing room.

Mackenzie stopped at the door. "I'm always ready. I never want to disappoint my audience."

"So far you're batting a thousand."

"That's all?" She couldn't help but think about Ian and his penchant for sport analogies.

"How about a million?" Julius offered.

She smiled. "That's more like it."

"Don't get too bigheaded. Even great singers have to work at it."

"I know that," she told him.

"You just keep remembering that, and you may have a future in this business."

"I'll do my best not to let you down."

Truthfully, Mackenzie wasn't sure what type of future she wanted as a jazz singer. She loved working as a stylist and couldn't imagine giving up her part of the business. She didn't believe Sophia would be too crazy about the idea, either. The notion of touring and dealing with the cutthroat record business was not something that had great appeal to Mackenzie. She loved singing for the artistic value and thrill of using her God-given talents in a way that made her and the audiences feel good.

Then there was the fact that paying homage to such legendary singers as Sarah Vaughan, Billie Holiday, Ella Fitzgerald, Dinah Washington, Lena Horne and June Christy was something Mackenzie felt honored to be able to do. What she wouldn't give to be able to step into any of their shoes.

A half hour later she had applied just enough makeup to add color to her face under the stage lights and changed into a crimson halter gown with black, ankle-strap sandals.

Mackenzie's piano man was Dorian Javier, a semiretired

musician who could still bring it home on the keys. They had clicked instantly and rarely seemed to miss the mark, making her job that much easier.

"Hey there, Lady Day," he said teasingly, borrowing Billie Holiday's nickname.

"I wish," she told him respectfully.

"You're doing more than wishing. The people out there are more excited about you than any of the other acts to step on this stage."

Mackenzie blushed. "I couldn't do it without you."

"Sure you could. These old bones won't be around forever. Whoever takes the keys will melt under your powerful vocals."

"If you say so."

"Don't take my word for it. Ask them out there and you'll hear the same thing time and time again."

Mackenzie beamed, knowing she felt just as highly about him. Which was why she was concerned about the pianist. In his mid-sixties, Dorian didn't look so good right now, though he hadn't indicated he was ill. But then, when did men ever come clean about medical issues? It was often left for women to assess instinctively. Maybe there was something wrong.

"So what do you want to do first?" Dorian got her attention.

She mentally went through the list of songs she'd perfected. "How about 'It Had To Be You'?"

He rubbed his nose. "Now, how could you ever go wrong with that one? Let's do it!"

Mackenzie sauntered to her spot before what looked to be a decent audience—the past few had been weak. Perhaps the tide was beginning to turn in her favor. Grabbing the microphone, she quelled the tiny bit of nerves that usually came every time she first took the stage.

She imagined the butterflies would really be churning in her stomach were Ian in the audience. He seemed like the type of man who would scrutinize every performance he attended. And probably wouldn't be afraid to tell the singer exactly what he thought for better or worse.

Of course, it still remained to be seen whether or not she and Ian had similar tastes in music, as well as other forms of artistic expression. Something told her they were much more alike than not. Only time would tell.

Mackenzie sucked in a calming breath, nodded at Dorian and began to sing. The audience seemed in it from the very start, which empowered her to give them a show they wouldn't soon forget. Dorian kept pace expertly, further boosting Mackenzie's confidence.

She absolutely loved lending her powerful vocals to a captive audience. It made her feel good, alive, spiritual and blessed. The experience literally lifted Mackenzie off her feet. The energy in there was palpable and she gave back everything she received, and then some.

On cue with Dorian, they moved right into "My Funny Valentine," followed by "Until the Real Thing Comes Along."

After her session ended, Mackenzie worked the audience. "Thank you," she said graciously, shaking hands and receiving plaudits. She realized that when in singing mode she had entered a whole new dimension where real and surreal blended effortlessly. She enjoyed the emotional high received from this and knew of nothing that could match it. But at the end of the day she was happy just being herself. A woman who was very down-to-earth and content to share that with a like-minded man such as Ian.

Ian woke up early, at five o'clock for a quick stroll with Otis. Then he showered, ate some cereal and was off to work.

He'd taken a job as a radio disc jockey with KRDQ in Cheri Village. The soft jazz station had made him an offer he simply couldn't refuse.

It hadn't been easy for Ian to leave Westport, where he'd made a life for himself and was generally happy with his job. But a change of scenery was in order with the arrival of new management and a change in the station's style of music. Aside from that, he'd recently ended a relationship that was going nowhere, so there had been no one in the romance department to keep him there.

So far Ian had no complaints with his new surroundings. They had warmly embraced him at the station and all members of the crew seemed like good people. On the home front there appeared to be promise with his wonderful new neighbor. There was definite chemistry between them and he was sure she felt it, too.

Still, Ian was content not to try and jump into anything with Mackenzie. He didn't want her to get the impression that it was all about sex with him. Yes, he had a powerful libido and looked for the same in a woman. But he also liked just chilling out and having fun. He wondered if Mackenzie was of the same mind. Or was she looking for an entirely different equation in a relationship?

Lost in thought, Ian arrived at the station.

"Looks like you could've used another hour of sleep," Doug Donahue, the news reporter, said with a chuckle.

"More like two." Ian yawned for effect. In fact, he loved doing the morning program. It allowed him to interact more with the audience and also left time during the day to spend with Otis and catch up on other things.

"You and me both. I made some fresh coffee. Better get a little bit in your system and you'll be good to go."

"I'll do that." Ian went into the coffee room, planning to

make himself a cup of green tea. He saw Emily Stewart, the traffic reporter, stirring cream into her mug.

She faced him, smiling. "Good morning."

"Morning."

Ian got a whiff of her strong perfume. She was in her mid-twenties and seemed to be attracted to him. Though a little flattered, he had no interest in her. He preferred a more mature woman, physically and mentally, to cozy up to.

A woman like Mackenzie Reese.

He walked around Emily. "Smooth sailing to work today as always for us early birds. What's on tap for the morning commute?"

She put the mug to her mouth and sipped her coffee before answering. "There's some downtown construction going on that will slow things down a bit. Other than that, same old same old, assuming there are no accidents."

"I'll keep my fingers crossed." Ian took out a tea bag and dropped it into his cup.

"So what's your question of the morning?" Emily asked.

"Hadn't really thought about it," he answered, usually waiting till the last moment to spring it on the listeners as a means to put some life into their commute. "I'm sure I'll come up with something to challenge them."

She nodded. "I agree. I think you've done a great job so far."

"It's what I was hired to do," Ian replied, flattered.

"That's true," Emily conceded.

"Speaking of, we'd better get out there and do our thing."

"Yeah, I suppose."

Ian turned away and grabbed his cup just as the perfect wake-up question popped into his head.

For an instant Mackenzie thought her mind must surely be playing tricks on her. The smooth voice with a touch of baritone she heard on the way to work couldn't possibly be her next-door neighbor.

But then no further doubt was left when he said, "Ian Kelly, coming to you live from KRDQ."

Mackenzie hadn't seen that coming. Ian said he was in communications, which could have meant any number of professions. A radio deejay hadn't been one she'd considered. Why hadn't he just said he was a disc jockey? Did he think it would matter to her?

Mackenzie was intrigued that Ian worked for a jazz station. Did this mean he loved the same kind of music she did? The notion excited her, even as she puzzled over his deception, if that was what it was.

She paid attention as he asked the listeners a question. "What is it about perennial gardens that make people so darn passionate about spending time in their backyards?"

Mackenzie laughed. If she hadn't known better she would think the question was directed at her. But how was that possible? Ian wouldn't have known that she listened to listen to KRDQ. Though she had never called into the show before, Mackenzie decided to go for it, not expecting to actually get through.

Then she heard on the radio, "I'm taking our first caller now. You're on the air with Ian Kelly."

"Is that me?" she asked into the speaker phone.

"You bet. And your name is?" The voice boomed from her phone and radio at the same time.

Mackenzie turned down the radio. *Don't you recognize my voice?*

"Let's just say I'm a woman who has a man in communications and his garden-loving dog as my neighbor. Will that suffice?"

Ian laughed. "Yeah, I think it will." He paused. "So what's your answer to the question?"

Mackenzie could hardly concentrate between driving and thinking about him.

"That's an easy one," she told him. "Gardening is a labor of love. You don't look at it as hard work, but rather the pure joy of watching the flowers you planted reach full bloom."

"Well put."

"Thank you."

"I doubt anyone could top that," Ian said.

Who was Mackenzie to argue the point? "Guess you'll have to wait and see what other callers have to say about the subject."

"Yeah. So will we hear from you again sometime?"

"Sure, if I have the answer to your question." Mackenzie disconnected on that note, giving him something to think about.

I have my own questions for you, Mr. Deejay. Will you be just as responsive?

Ian chuckled to himself after taking another call. In fact, he'd been hoping that Mackenzie might be out there listening to his morning chatter. But hoping and believing were two different things.

Then, just like that, she'd called in. He'd been thrown initially, as her voice was slightly altered from using a speaker phone. But even then Mackenzie managed to give him a warm feeling in their brief exchange. He could imagine warm turning to red-hot, should they ever take things to the next level.

After listening to three other callers give their take on gardening, Ian had had enough.

"I think I've had my question answered by our caller experts in gardening," he told the listeners. "The first caller, in particular, seemed to sum things up rather nicely, so why don't we try a little Frank Sinatra singing one of his classic tunes, 'Strangers in the Night.'"

Ian played the song and wondered when he might hear from Mackenzie again on the show.

"So who's the mystery lady?" Doug asked, off the air from his control room.

Ian thought about pleading the Fifth on that one, but decided to come clean. "My next-door neighbor."

"What was that whole garden-dog thing about?"

"My dog made the mistake of getting into her flower garden."

Doug laughed. "I bet that went over well."

"I guarantee you she thought it was anything but funny."

"I assume you've since kissed and made up?"

The kissing will come in time. Ian could almost taste her lips and was sure they would be worth the wait.

"Something like that."

"So she's single, then?" Doug asked.

"Very much so."

"Well, I guess you'll keep us updated if anything comes out of this neighborly banter?"

Ian wasn't particularly interested in sharing his love life over the airwaves. But he saw no harm in satisfying Doug's curiosity, should things heat up with Mackenzie.

"Count on it," he said, just before the song by Ol' Blue Eyes ended.

Chapter 8

"I can't believe Ian Kelly lives right next door to you!" Mackenzie's friend Estelle said while Mackenzie was putting in her extensions.

"Believe it." She smiled, though a little miffed that Ian had kept it from her that he was a radio personality.

"KRDQ is my favorite station these days—especially after KPTN went off the air."

"I'll be sure to pass that along to Ian," joked Mackenzie.

"He's got the sexiest voice—aside from Talbot."

"Better keep your eye on the ball, girlfriend."

Estelle laughed. "Talbot knows I love him, but nothing says I can't look every now and then."

"You mean listen, don't you?"

"That, too." She adjusted in the chair. "So have you gotten to know your sexy-voiced neighbor any better yet or what?"

Certainly not as well as I'd like to. "We've played a little basketball and exchanged pleasantries. That's about it," Mackenzie said, trying to hide her smile.

"Does Ian look as good as he sounds?"

"Every bit," Mackenzie admitted dreamily.

"Sounds like someone has a crush on her neighbor," Estelle teased.

"Perhaps it's the other way around…."

"Is he single?"

"Yes." Mackenzie tried to concentrate on what she was doing, but Estelle wasn't making it easy.

"Hmm…so maybe he's what's been occupying your thoughts these days?" she suggested.

"Right now, you're the one occupying my thoughts," Mackenzie said stiffly. "Now will you keep your head down?"

"I'll take that as a yes!"

"Take it any way you like." Mackenzie was used to her meddlesome but well-meaning friends. That didn't mean she had to divulge every bit of news about who she was interested in. At least not until there was something concrete to report back.

"I'll do that." Estelle bent her head back as instructed. "Have you told Mr. Jazz Deejay that you sing?"

"Not yet." Though she might have, had she known his true profession.

"Well, I'm sure it will leave a favorable impression on him."

Would it? She wasn't sure. She could never measure up against some of the true giants of jazz he played on the radio.

"I'd rather he were more impressed with who I am inside than how I sound."

"Spoken like someone who hasn't gotten any in a while," snickered Estelle.

"I want to be with a man," Mackenzie admitted, "but he still has to be into *me,* first and foremost."

* * *

When she got home that evening, Mackenzie felt worn down. The clients had seemed to come nonstop and were particularly demanding. She was ready to grab a quick bite to eat and go to bed. But seeing Ian's car in his driveway and remembering the surprise of hearing him on the radio, she decided to ask him about their chat that morning.

Mackenzie walked up to his door and heard Otis barking. She was still trying to figure out if the dog liked her or not. She was more than willing to meet him halfway, so long as he left her garden alone. She didn't necessarily believe a dog was the key to a man's heart, but supposed it wouldn't hurt her cause if she became friends with Otis.

The door opened and a bare-chested Ian came into view.

"Hey there," he said with a wide grin.

The mere sight of his glistening muscular arms, broad chest and six-pack abs left Mackenzie speechless.

When she found her voice, it was uneven but to the point.

"Why didn't you tell me what you did for a living?"

He scratched his head. "I thought I had."

Mackenzie batted her lashes. "Communications?"

A smile played on his lips again. "Well, that's pretty much the size of it."

She glanced again at his muscled frame and back to his steady eyes. "You'll have to do better than that."

"All right, I will. Would you like to come in?"

Mackenzie was ready to seize the opportunity, not only to learn more about him, but to see what things looked like inside his house.

"Sure," she told him.

Ian stepped aside. When Mackenzie passed him, he nostrils inhaled the combined scent of his cologne and natural manly smell that she found incredibly attractive.

After walking through the foyer, she entered the huge living room. At first glance, Mackenzie saw designer furniture and a framed scenic oil painting. Her eyes did a double take when she spotted a white baby grand piano near vaulted windows.

She turned to Ian and asked, "You play the piano?"

"Used to," he said, "I guess I mainly keep it around to help fill out the room."

"Why did you stop playing?"

He grabbed a short-sleeved, ecru shirt from a swivel rocker and put it on. "I just got tired of it."

Mackenzie's eyes widened. "Who gets tired of having such a talent?"

"Someone who realized his strengths were more suited toward giving much more talented musicians their chance to shine."

Mackenzie thought about the artists he played at the station. "So you were about to tell me why you never mentioned you were a deejay."

"Yeah, that. Well, I never go out of my way to bring it up. Some people make a big deal out of being a radio personality. I wanted you to get to know me first as your neighbor and any other way we came to define our relationship."

Did he really see them as having a relationship?

"But you almost seemed to know that I'd call in for your question…"

He chuckled. "You struck me as someone who could appreciate jazz. I rolled the dice and there you were."

"Lucky you."

"Lucky us." He grinned. "Seems like you were a big hit this morning. Apparently there are a lot more gardeners in Vermont than I realized. And most agreed with you wholeheartedly."

That gave Mackenzie a warm feeling. "I suppose it takes one to know one."

"I'm not so sure about that. Last I knew, I didn't have a gardening bone in my body," he said as he moved closer. "But I certainly do know someone who has...and I'm liking her more with each passing day."

"Is that so?"

"Yes, it is."

She met his eyes, which were bearing down on her with such intensity that Mackenzie felt her knees shake. She wanted—needed—him to kiss her.

"And what are you going to do about it?" she asked boldly.

Ian put his arms around her waist. "Something I've wanted to do again for a while now...."

Tilting his head slightly, he kissed her. It was slow and deliberate, gentle without being too soft and firm but with conviction.

The kiss was more than enough to get Mackenzie's attention. She felt light on her feet and giddy. Caught up in the moment, her arms made their way around Ian's neck. She didn't want this moment to end.

Apparently Ian didn't either as he held her tighter and opened his mouth to take in more of hers. Mackenzie was happy to give in to his urgency, as hers was just as demanding. The kiss seemed to go on and on as her body temperature rose in response. Mackenzie wasn't sure she could ever remember another time that she had been kissed like this. The man definitely knew what he was doing.

Mackenzie considered herself a pretty good kisser, too, and she went for it, loving the idea of her lips being entwined with someone so virile and polished. Even his taste was making her smolder with desire.

One of her hands slipped to his bald head, holding on to it firmly as if to keep Ian from getting away. Not that he was in a hurry to leave this wonderful moment. After a while Mackenzie had lost all concept of time and space, so engrossed was she in the kiss and with Ian's fervor. By now their mouths were interlocked in a perfect fit of succulent smooching, tongue twirling and soul searching, leaving Mackenzie exhausted while still wanting desperately to take this to the next level. She was pretty sure that Ian shared her feelings. When he pulled away, Mackenzie felt as though it were mental telepathy.

Ian licked his lips. "That was amazing."

"Yes, it was," she freely admitted, already thinking of what they should do for an encore.

"I could definitely get used to that."

"Me, too." Mackenzie touched her swollen mouth.

Ian grinned. "Do you want to grab a bite to eat?"

Her eyes blinked. "Now…?"

"Yeah," Ian said as he nodded. "I was planning to try a place recommended by a coworker and would love some company."

Mackenzie had worked up an appetite, too, but not for food. Why was he holding back?

Maybe he has willpower like few other men I've known and really does want to get to know me better as a woman rather than in bed. How can I find fault in that?

Besides, since this would be their first date, Mackenzie quickly warmed to the idea.

"Well, I am hungry," she told him.

"Great. So am I."

"Give me fifteen minutes to change."

"You've got it."

Mackenzie glanced at the piano, if only to take her mind off her lips, which still burned from his kiss. She hated to see such a magnificent instrument go to waste.

"Do you think I could get you to play something for me one day?"

He ran a hand across his chin, eyes twinkling. "You could probably get me to do just about anything you wanted."

Mackenzie had a mind to test that notion right now as she wanted him badly in the physical sense. But she put that thought on hold.

"I'll keep that in mind."

It took every ounce of willpower Ian had to keep from pouncing on Mackenzie like a leopard. The kiss they shared was much more passionate than he'd anticipated, arousing his mental and physical senses. Making love to her would, no doubt, be every bit as explosive and satisfying.

Maybe tonight, he thought. But for the moment, he was content to savor the memory of her sweet kiss and look forward to Mackenzie's company for dinner.

He took her to a quaint restaurant that overlooked the Lamoille River. Ian was impressed with the decor, but not half as much as he was with Mackenzie. She had changed into a low-cut, rose-colored blouse and heather-gray cropped pants with a pair of taupe pumps to complete the outfit.

Ian could barely take his eyes off her as they sat across from each other in a booth while waiting for the food to arrive.

"Have you ever been here before?" he asked.

"No. It's a bit expensive for my budget."

"You don't strike me as needing to be too budget-conscious." After all, she lived in an upper-middle-class neighborhood, was gainfully employed and didn't have the extra financial burden of taking care of a teenager. Was he missing something in the equation?

She met his eyes. "I never said I needed to be. I just choose to be. It helps me stay on top of the bottom line as a single woman."

"Probably a smart thing in this day and age, single or not."

"But that doesn't mean I want to leave and go to McDonald's instead."

Ian laughed. He liked her sense of humor, something that had been decidedly lacking in his former girlfriends. But did that mean he already considered Mackenzie to be his girlfriend, or was he being presumptuous?

"I think we'll stay here and splurge a bit," he said. "Besides, you're worth every penny."

"How can you be so sure?"

"My instincts rarely fail me."

"I see," she said and grinned. "I like your instincts."

"And I like you." Ian lifted his wine. "So I guess we're even."

"Sounds good to me." She raised her own glass.

Ian watched as she tasted the wine and licked her lips. He couldn't wait to taste the fullness of her mouth again. Only this time he wanted to delve much further into the physical attraction between them.

The waitress brought their food. Mackenzie had ordered shrimp scampi over linguini. It sounded great and prompted Ian to follow suit.

"I take it you worked as a deejay in Connecticut, too?" Mackenzie asked.

"You take it right." Ian dabbed the napkin to his lips. "Been doing this for the past twelve years."

"And before that?"

He went for the wine. "I freelanced on the piano for various artists."

She favored him with interest. "Anyone I might have heard of?"

"Probably not. It was mostly on the small-club circuit and college campuses. Not particularly glamorous, or the stuff riches are made of, but it was steady income."

"Obviously being a deejay is something you're comfortable with then?" Mackenzie questioned as she grabbed a dinner roll.

Ian nodded. "It's a cool way to bring music to the public and have a little fun in the process." He met her gaze. "How long have you been a fan of jazz?"

"Since my Mom first introduced me to Sarah Vaughan, Nancy Wilson and Billie Holiday," Mackenzie said.

"Can't go wrong with any of those legendary singers."

"Not one bit. I love the standards, swing, Latin jazz, even some of the new stuff."

It excited Ian to meet someone with a true appreciation of jazz music.

"I also sing jazz," Mackenzie said nonchalantly.

"You mean like in the shower?"

"That, too." She laughed. "I perform at a club every other Saturday."

Ian cocked a brow. "Really?"

"It's something I've wanted to do for a long time and now I finally have the opportunity."

"Looks like we've both got hidden talents," Ian said with a smile.

"Mine are not exactly hidden," she pointed out. "If I'd known you were a deejay on a jazz station from day one, I'm sure I would've shared the fact that I sing with you."

Ian went along with that. He was even more impressed with her. "I'd love to watch your show."

She smiled. "Then you're invited."

"Is it a club in town?"

"Burlington."

Ian immediately thought of his friend, Julius Garrison, who had a lounge there.

"What's it called?"

"Deer Lounge," Mackenzie said. "Have you heard of it?"

"As a matter of fact, I have." He grinned. "I went to college with your boss, Julius."

She looked shocked. "You're kidding."

"Nope. We both played in a small band back in the day. We weren't really very good as a unit, but we had fun."

Mackenzie's eyes twinkled. "You're just full of surprises."

"We both are." He lifted his wine glass, imagining her as a jazz vocalist. "Helps keep things lively."

"I'll say." She chuckled.

Ian grabbed the bill. "Are you ready to go?"

"Yes, I am. Thank you for dinner. The food was excellent."

He hoped there was a scrumptious dessert in store for both of them.

"Would you like to come in for a nightcap?" Mackenzie offered, after Ian walked her up to the door. She tried not to be too obvious or to appear desperate.

She wanted Ian, plain and simple. But he had to want her just as much if they were to take the next step in this romance.

"I'd love to," he responded without missing a beat.

The moment they stepped inside the door, Mackenzie turned on the light and then faced Ian. She searched the depths of his eyes until finding what she was looking for—an unbridled hunger that matched her own.

Without waiting for him to make the first move, Mackenzie grabbed his cheeks and reached up for a mouthwatering kiss. It was every bit as intense as their last kiss, only even more demanding. She could feel the pressure in Ian's pants fighting to break through his clothing. The thought of him being inside her left Mackenzie excited beyond words. Her breasts brushed against his chest, sending a jolt through her body and making Mackenzie eager to feel Ian's strong hands all over her.

As if he'd read her thoughts, Ian wrapped his arms around Mackenzie and flattened her mouth with his in their most powerful kiss yet. She tasted his tongue, still sweet like grapes from the wine. Mackenzie clung to Ian. She had been tilted practically off her feet, but she felt as if she were floating on air. She had no doubt that with Ian's size and strength she was safe from falling.

Except for the man himself.

"I want to make love to you," he murmured huskily.

"Then we both want the same thing," she cooed, as she un-buttoned his shirt.

He began simultaneously opening her blouse. "You're so beautiful."

"So are you." Mackenzie again found herself admiring his naked chest and flat stomach. Now she wanted to see the rest. They managed to make their way into the living room before all their clothes were shed and they were both naked.

Whatever shyness Mackenzie may have felt in exposing herself to her neighbor was overcome by the magnificent sight he presented and the fact that she knew he was just as impressed with her body.

"Do you want to go upstairs?" she asked.

Ian put his hands on her waist. "Yes, later. But I'd rather have you right here and now, to start."

Mackenzie felt a tingle of anticipation. She sank down onto the sofa and watched Ian follow. He brought his mouth down upon hers, and their lips locked lustfully. She circled her tongue around inside his mouth, totally caught up in the foreplay and wanting to discover every small detail there was about him.

Ian caressed her nipples, making Mackenzie want to scream with delight. He seemed to enjoy torturing her, spend-ing an endless amount of time teasing and stimulating her breasts while still maintaining their kiss. Mackenzie basked in his attention, even as she felt a new wave of pleasure com-ing when Ian's hand slid down her body and found a place between her legs. He began to stimulate her there, causing her whole body to blaze with desire.

"Oh…Ian." She bit her lip, trying not to climax too soon.

"Just relax," he whispered, "and let me satisfy you."

"I'm all yours."

"Yes, you are…."

Ian was turned on as never before when he kissed Mackenzie passionately. As he caressed her body she reacted to his touch as if it burned her skin. That told him all he needed to know about where they'd be heading.

He unlocked his lips from Mackenzie's and began to kiss her eyelids, cheeks, chin, ears and neck. He slowly moved down her chest until he reached her breasts. They were perfect—full and rounded with nipples erect from arousal. He licked one and heard Mackenzie gasp, inspiring him to continue longer before moving on to the other.

She trembled. "You're killing me—"

"And you're bringing me to life," he countered, sucking her nipples until they hardened.

Ian's erection throbbed, but he fought the need to gratify it just yet. First he wanted to get Mackenzie wetter than she already was. He planted kisses down her stomach and rolled his lips across her smooth flesh until he arrived at the essence of Mackenzie's womanhood. Ian tasted her moist vaginal lips, aroused by the scent. He wanted to claim her and more. He started to lick her clitoris, circling several times before zooming in with ardor. Mackenzie's moans and quivers worked their magic on him and Ian took delight in getting very familiar with this part of her.

"Make love to me," Mackenzie uttered. "Please!"

Given that he could barely contain himself as it was, Ian was only too happy to oblige. He lifted himself from between her legs and looked her in the eyes.

"With pleasure," he said. He grabbed a condom from his pants pocket and slid it on himself before slowly getting between her waiting legs. Ian then entered Mackenzie with passion, finding her a tight, wet fit. She immediately wrapped her legs around him and absorbed his powerful thrusts, giving back as much as she took.

He brought his mouth down on hers and they kissed with utter abandon. The taste of Mackenzie on Ian's lips drove him mad with hunger. He pulled her up and, while on his knees, continued to make love to Mackenzie. She clawed his back and nibbled on his ears. He kissed her breasts and stroked her buttocks. Both were drenched in perspiration, moving in perfect harmony as though having been intimate for years.

When Ian felt his surge approaching, he laid Mackenzie back down so that he could go even deeper inside her. They clasped hands as he quickened his fluid thrusts. Both were breathing irregularly while Ian's heart pounded loudly in his ears.

"Don't stop," gasped Mackenzie, her body arching as she clamped around Ian.

"I wouldn't think of it," he spoke in a husky voice and tried to catch his breath.

He fought back the urge to climax, not wanting to do so before Mackenzie. Instead Ian focused on relishing the feel of their being together so intimately, exploring each other and already looking toward the next round.

Mackenzie bit his lip while shuddering wildly and Ian took this as his cue and picked up the pace, wanting to catch up to her so they could experience the moment together. The pleasure reverberated throughout Ian's body, leaving him exhausted, but satisfied. They held each other tightly as the frenzied moment waned and their equilibriums returned to normal.

Ian kissed Mackenzie's lips soulfully. After a few moments he asked, "Shall we take it upstairs for another round?"

She kissed him back heartily. "I'm ready if you are."

That was all he needed to hear.

Mackenzie held Ian's hand while leading him into her bedroom. A fresh wave of desire rippled through her body. He was bringing to the surface raw needs that she'd buried for a long time. Now she wanted to explore them to their fullest while giving in to Ian's passionate demands.

Ian turned to Mackenzie with a look of lust as he said, "I'm quickly discovering I can't get enough of you."

She felt the same way, which made her feel both scared and delighted.

Ian laid Mackenzie on the bed and gave her a long, probing kiss that left her breathless. His face moved to the valley between her breasts where he licked around slowly before turning his attention to her nipples, sucking and running his tongue across one and then the other and back, increasing the intensity over time. Once again, this brought Mackenzie to the brink of coming. She bit her tongue and fought the urge, wanting to prolong his exquisite foreplay for as long as she could.

Ian began to move downward and put his face between her thighs. His mouth began nibbling at the insides of her legs, before honing in directly between them, licking fervently, sending waves of pleasure coursing through Mackenzie. She moved her head from side to side, caught up thoroughly in the moment of delightful agony. She realized that she couldn't hold out any longer, so powerful was his oral stimulation.

Mackenzie squeezed Ian between her legs, holding on tightly as the moment of ecstasy gripped her like a fever. A guttural moan left her throat as she climaxed, moving up and down on his mouth shamelessly.

Still caught in the throes of desire, Mackenzie sucked in a deep breath.

"Now let's do that together," Ian uttered when he lifted his head up.

"Yes, let's." Mackenzie desperately moved her body down the bed to meet with his.

Ian slipped on another condom and moved himself between Mackenzie's legs. He went in easily and deeply. Mackenzie splayed her legs wide and absorbed each potent thrust with sweet surrender.

"Kiss me!" she demanded, wanting to feel every inch of him on her.

He obeyed, bringing his mouth down to hers with sizzling heat. Wanting him to go deeper, Mackenzie brought her legs up, bending her knees until they were close to her face. She grabbed Ian's buttocks, urging him on, pushing her groin against his. Ian responded to her plea, moving into her with sustained determination. Their wet bodies clung together and their mouths locked while their tongues searched deeply for satisfaction.

Mackenzie felt a surge of heat between her legs when the climax came, quickly spreading out to every part of her body. She cried out raggedly, clawing Ian's back unmercifully, desperate to maintain the overwhelming sensation of fulfillment. Five more minutes passed of intense lovemaking as Mackenzie absorbed Ian's penetration until he, too, found satisfaction.

He fell onto her afterwards, still wedged inside as both fought to catch their breaths. Mackenzie held Ian's slick bald head to her breasts while her legs stretched across his buttocks, pinning them together. She wished they could stay like that forever, caught in their own world of erotic pleasure and sexual bonding.

Then there was the emotional element of their lovemaking. Mackenzie could not have sex like they had without developing feelings for her lover. She just hadn't figured out how she felt yet. She only knew that Ian was very special to her and she didn't want that feeling go away anytime soon. She only hoped that Ian felt the same.

Ian pulled out of her slowly, kissing Mackenzie's forehead. "That was fun."

"Just fun?"

"Spectacularly fun and insanely pleasurable."

"Will you hold me?" Mackenzie hoped she wasn't scaring him off with the request, aware that most men had little desire for cuddling after sex.

"I'd love to hold you."

She faced him and he brought her closer, kissing and embracing her with his muscular arms.

Mackenzie smelled the sweet scent of their sex all over their bodies, arousing her. It seemed as if she couldn't get enough of Ian. She envisioned making love to him every day. But she didn't dare look too far ahead, fearing she could be setting herself up for a fall.

Having twice before made the mistake of becoming attracted to the wrong man, this time she would move forward with more caution and hope that what was developing between them would sort itself out properly. As Mackenzie thought about all of this, her eyes grew heavy. She fell asleep in Ian's arms, dreaming about him and how being neighbors had suddenly become so much more. When she awakened, Mackenzie found it was the middle of the night. She was alone in bed.

Ian was gone.

Chapter 9

Ian was up bright and early to take Otis out before heading to work. He'd wanted nothing more than to spend every night like the last. He wanted to be with Mackenzie, having so enjoyed their afternoon of conversation and lovemaking.

But he wasn't sure if they were quite ready to begin regular sleepovers. As such, he decided it was best to return home after Mackenzie introduced him to her bed and into her life in a way that was better than he ever could have hoped for.

"Are you about done?" Ian asked Otis, who seemed to take his sweet time in relieving himself against some bushes.

When Ian returned home, he saw the light on in Mackenzie's bedroom. A spark of desire hit him in that instant as he had a flashback to the passion they'd shared. He had a mind to pop over for some morning fun, but wasn't sure she was up to it. Though if last night were any indication, he'd met his perfect match in the bedroom.

I'll resist temptation and save it for another time.

Ian went inside his house and let Otis loose, then hopped into the shower. Half an hour later he was at the station.

"How are you this morning?" Emily said over her shoulder as Ian sat down.

"Terrific."

"Any reason in particular?" She chuckled. "Or is it because you get to see me?"

Ian laughed uneasily. She was flirting with him. No harm, no foul, he thought.

"It's always nice to see you, Emily. And it's even nicer when I get to breathe in the morning fresh air and greet my listeners warmly."

"At least you're honest. Can't say that for all men."

"I'm not every other man."

"I can see that." She moved so he could see her face. "Guess that's what I like about you."

"Listen, I think you're a great girl I enjoy working with—"

Emily cut him off. "Hey, I'm not hitting on you."

"Really?"

"Yes, really. I'm like this with everyone. You'll just have to get used to it."

"Thanks for the warning."

Emily flashed a smile and left his booth.

Ian wasn't quite sure what to make of her. What he did know was that the only woman occupying his thoughts these days was Mackenzie.

"Morning, folks," he told his listeners, wondering if Mackenzie was among them. "Hope you've had your cup of coffee or tea and are ready to tackle a new day. I've got just the right mellow jazz to get you started…"

* * *

"You are positively glowing, girlfriend," remarked Sophia at the salon.

Mackenzie batted her eyes. "Am I?"

"Something tells me that things must be heating up between you and Mr. Neighbor Deejay…"

"Well, if you must know, we *are* becoming better acquainted…"

"So in other words, you slept with him?" Sophia pressed.

Mackenzie regarded her thoughtfully. "I wouldn't exactly call what we were doing sleeping."

Sophia laughed. "I knew it!"

"Knew what?" Lynda, one of the stylists, came from the back room.

"Mackenzie has herself a man."

"Anyone I know?"

"Only if you listen to KRDQ, which is all about jazz."

Lynda wrinkled her nose. "Sorry, I'm more into hip-hop and soul."

"I won't hold that against you," Mackenzie said, wondering if Ian really was her man. The man was forty years old and never married. Was he even looking for a steady girlfriend?

"It's cool, though, that you're into someone."

"I second that," Sophia said. "Why should we have all the fun, while you're left wondering if your social life is over?"

"I never felt that way." Mackenzie stood her ground. "I was happy with my life."

"*Was* is the operative word. Maybe now you can make that 'ecstatic'!"

"I wouldn't put the cart ahead of the horse just yet," Mackenzie stated. "We're not at the ecstatic stage at this point."

Maybe they were in bed, she conceded, a tiny shiver enveloping her at the thought of Ian's tongue making its way to every crevice of her body. But a relationship required more than just sex. Whether Ian was prepared for a greater commitment was still unclear.

"Well, as soon as you get that stallion tamed, be sure to let us know," Sophia quipped.

Lynda pretended to ride a horse, causing Mackenzie to laugh. She had no problem with the teasing from her friends and colleagues. It was all in good fun. They also wanted to see her add substance to the blessed life she already had. Ian did just that and more.

"I will," she told them, though not sure if Ian was tamable. "Right now, we have to get ready for our customers."

Still, Mackenzie knew that Ian would never be very far from her mind.

Chapter 10

"Good to see you again," Ian said, shaking the hand of his college friend Julius Garrison.

"You too, man." Julius sported a goatee and was impeccably dressed in a double-breasted designer suit. "You haven't changed a bit."

"I only wish that were true." Ian grinned and sat back on the leather sectional. He had finally taken the time to visit his friend's impressive lakefront Georgian home.

"Guess we've both come a long way."

"Yeah. Hopefully we're just getting warmed up."

Julius laughed. "I hear you."

Ian's gaze shifted to see his friend's wife, Yasmine, who approached them with martinis in her hands.

"There you are." She handed one to each of them.

"Thanks." Ian surveyed her. Yasmine was in her early thirties, petite and busty with shoulder-length, straight, burgundy hair.

She sat beside her husband. "Julius was just telling me a little bit about you."

"Oh, really?" Ian said. "Anything more and you might never have let me in the front door."

She giggled. "Sense of humor, too. I find that very sexy in a man."

"Uh-oh." Julius leaned forward, eyes widening. "Do I need to be worried here, old buddy?"

"I don't think so." Ian assumed he was just kidding. "You obviously have a lovely wife and I couldn't be happier for you both."

Julius grinned. "Hey, I'm just playing with you. Yasmine's a natural flirt. We both are. Keeps things lively."

"Whatever works." Ian tasted the drink.

Yasmine licked her lips. "I heard you on the radio."

"Is that right?"

"I think you bring energy to the morning program."

"Thanks." Ian couldn't help but like her, flirting aside.

"He was the same way when we played music together in college," Julius said. "Ian's passion for what we were doing kept us together."

"Do you still play?" Yasmine asked.

"Not really. That phase of my life is pretty much over." Ian wondered at times if he had given up too soon on a career in music. Perhaps the few bad breaks in his early career were not an indicator of his talents, but of his lack of connections with the right people.

"When are you coming to the club?" Julius looked at him.

"I'll try to make it out there real soon." Ian thought about Mackenzie. "Speaking of which, seems like we have more in common than our long-standing friendship."

"Oh?" Julius lifted a brow.

"Your singer, Mackenzie Reese, happens to be my next-door neighbor." *And so much more,* he thought.

"Mackenzie never mentioned—"

"We only put two and two together yesterday."

"That's incredible." Julius shook his head. "I mean, what are the odds?"

"I know."

"Have you heard her sing?" Yasmine widened her eyes.

"Not yet."

"You don't know what you're missing," Julius said confidently. "The lady can really work those pipes! She sings with the kind of poise and confidence that many seasoned singers don't have."

Ian could only imagine. He felt envious that Julius had experienced a part of Mackenzie that he had not.

"I can't wait to hear her for myself."

"And she's gorgeous, too," Yasmine added.

"I agree." Ian loved looking at Mackenzie for that very reason. Kissing her was even better, not to mention the other forms of intimacy they had engaged in. The thought made Ian smile.

"Am I sensing something here?" Julius narrowed his eyes.

"Meaning?"

"That there's more going on between you and Mackenzie than just neighborly friendship."

Ian's smile widened. To his old friend he saw no reason to downplay his budding relationship.

"We've started seeing each other." He felt it was reasonable to assume they had become an item, so it really wasn't much of an exaggeration.

"That's nice," Yasmine chimed in. "You two make a great couple."

"Thanks." Ian sat back, feeling good about things between him and Mackenzie. "We get along well."

"I can see that," Julius said, lifting his glass. "No wonder you've taken yourself off the market."

"Yeah, I'm looking forward to seeing how things develop in our relationship." He certainly had no complaints at this point. Mackenzie was a real woman with many layers that Ian looked forward to uncovering.

"Have you met her son?"

"Not yet. He's living in L.A. with his father."

"I'd heard that. Hope he doesn't rain on your parade anytime soon."

"I don't see that happening."

"Neither did I with my last wife." Julius grimaced. "Then just like that, suddenly I'm playing daddy to her brat pack from hell."

Ian's lips twisted. He hadn't thought too much about Mackenzie's son. There was no reason to believe he would be showing up for anything other than a visit, which Ian could deal with. Though he was happy without children in his life, Mackenzie's son would always be a part of her and he had to accept that.

Still, Ian was happy having Mackenzie all to himself for now. And it was clear she was just as happy giving all of herself to him.

When Mackenzie got home, she didn't see Ian's car. There had been no contact since he had climbed out of her bed in the wee hours of the morning, leaving her naked and longing for more of him. She didn't make too much of it, especially since he clearly enjoyed being with her as much as she did with him.

She would let him make the first move. Until then, she could savor the memories and anticipate what lay ahead.

Mackenzie grabbed a bottled water from the fridge and drank some before calling Ryan. She hoped things had settled down between him and his stepmother. But what if they hadn't? Could she really stay on the sidelines if her ex-husband's new wife was making Ryan's life miserable?

She got Ryan's voice mail. "Hi, honey. Haven't heard from you in a while. Give me a call when you can and let me know what's happening. Love you."

Mackenzie disconnected and decided on the spur of the moment to call her ex. They had spoken very little since their marriage ended, except where it concerned Ryan. She liked it better that way, having little to say to the man who betrayed her trust and loyalty.

"This is a surprise." Brent's voice on the line sounded as if it weren't an altogether pleasant one.

"I was trying to reach Ryan. Do you know where he is?"

"I suppose he's hanging out with friends."

"Don't you know for sure?" she questioned. "What if something happened to him?"

"He's fine." Brent's voice thickened. "What is this really about?"

"It's about me sending our son to live with you. I'm trusting you to take good care of him."

"That's what I'm doing. The fact that I can't account for his whereabouts twenty-four-seven hardly means I'm being a bad parent."

Mackenzie curled her lip. "Never said you were. Just a bad husband—at least with me."

She hated sounding like a bitter ex-wife. Especially since they had both moved on.

"That's water under the bridge."

"If you say so." Mackenzie did not want to see this turn into a trip down memory lane.

"How are things your way?" He cleared his throat. "Or am I not allowed to ask that?"

"Things are fine," she was glad to report.

"That's good to know."

"Is it really?"

He gave a terse chuckle. "Believe it or not, I want you to be happy, just as I am."

"Well, right now I'm more concerned about Ryan being happy out there," Mackenzie admitted.

"He is," Brent insisted. "Has he told you otherwise?"

She wanted to be careful not to get Ryan in trouble. But she also felt the need to make sure he was being given a fair shake. "No. Is he getting along well with your wife?"

Brent paused. "They're having an adjustment period."

"But he's been living there for more than six months. How much adjusting do they need?"

"I can't answer that. All I can say is that he's my son and she's my wife. We'll make it work."

"I hope so."

"Are you saying you want him back?"

She considered the question. Between her jobs and the new man in her life—a man with an aversion to kids—Mackenzie saw no reason to change the status quo.

"I want him where he wants to be," she responded. "If it's on the West Coast with his father, I'm not going to try to make him change his mind."

"Good." There was a moment of silent awkwardness. "I'll tell him you called."

"I left a voice mail." She cleared her throat. "I have to go."

"See you."

Mackenzie saw that she had a text message from Ryan. After disconnecting Brent, she read it:

Hey, Mom. Got msg. I'm OK. Later. R.

She smiled, deciding not to get overly worried right now about his welfare.

Mackenzie heard a car and peeked out the window. It was Ian pulling into his driveway. She got butterflies wondering if he would stop by.

Ian rang Mackenzie's bell. Fresh thoughts of the previous night rolled through his head, making him eager to experience even more of her tonight. *Was she having the same thoughts?*

Mackenzie opened the door, looking as sexy as ever in a sleeveless black-and-white polka-dot dress.

"Hey," he said.

"Hey yourself." She met his eyes searchingly.

"I'm going to barbecue some ribs and chicken. I was hoping you'd join me."

Her lips curved upward. "Sounds tasty. I'd love to."

He smiled back. "Good. They should be finger-licking ready before you know it."

"Can hardly wait."

"Neither can I."

She gave him a dreamy look that said *kiss me.* Ian found it hard to resist. He tilted his head and brought his mouth down to hers for a long, soft kiss. He loved the taste of Mackenzie as their open lips pressed together.

It was with reluctance that Ian pulled back. Otherwise he might never get around to firing up the grill and feeding them actual food.

Mackenzie ran her pinky across his moist mouth. "That was nice."

He touched his lower lip that was still tingling. "There's much more where it came from."

"I would have been disappointed if that was not the case."

He grinned. "See you shortly."

Ian went back to his house and let Otis out in the yard before grabbing the charcoal bag. This would be the first time he'd used his new gas grill. The fact that he was breaking it in with a special guest made the experience all the more pleasurable. He'd prepared the meat the way his parents had taught him, letting it marinate in the fridge. As soon as the coals were ready, he put the meat on the grill. Otis quickly came over with a hopeful look.

"Sorry, it's not for you, boy," he said. "But I promise you'll be well fed, too. Just be sure you're on your best behavior for Mackenzie."

He had no doubt that would be the case. Otis had not only warmed up to Mackenzie, but Ian sensed the dog understood there was something going on between her and his owner. Their new relationship demanded Otis accept her as one of their pack.

Ian went back inside to prepare the rest of the meal.

Mackenzie was happy she hadn't yet eaten by herself as she much preferred Ian's and Otis's company for dinner. She took the liberty of making some fresh lemonade for the occasion. She decided to bring a bottle of wine over to Ian's, as well.

She suspected that as a single man, Ian was probably not used to cooking. She certainly didn't want to cramp his style or try and take over. But on second thought, after having a husband who seemed to have trouble even pouring cereal into a bowl, it was refreshing to know the man was at least comfortable around a grill.

She walked into Ian's backyard where he stood over the shiny, red barbecue, Otis at his side. The appealing aroma of barbecued ribs and chicken filled her nostrils. Her gaze drifted to a white cedar picnic table that had already been set with two bowls of food on it.

Otis ran toward her and barked once as the welcoming committee, before running back toward Ian.

He gave her a big grin. "Right on time."

"I always try to be." She smiled. "Doesn't hurt when you only have to walk next door."

Ian laughed. "Being neighbors does have its benefits."

Mackenzie's pulse quickened as she considered the meaning of his words.

"I brought drinks."

He glanced at the lemonade and wine. "Thanks."

She put them on the table. "Anything else I can do?"

"I forgot the napkins. They're in the first drawer next to the fridge."

"I'll take care of it." Mackenzie loved that he had no problem accepting her help. The man seemed almost too good to be true.

She went through the side door and up three steps to a gourmet kitchen. Mackenzie passed by a commercial-grade, six-burner stove and French-door refrigerator before opening the drawer and getting the napkins.

Fifteen minutes later they were eating.

"It's delicious," Mackenzie said after tasting a tender rib and licking her fingers.

Ian chuckled with amusement. "I'm glad you like it." He dug his teeth into a chicken thigh. "That makes two of us."

She took delight in watching him eat. A small amount of barbecue sauce had clung to the corner of his mustache. It turned her on as she imagined licking it off.

"I saw Julius this afternoon," Ian said, dabbing a napkin on his mouth.

"Oh…?" Mackenzie's lashes fluttered. "I'm sure he was surprised to hear that we're neighbors."

"Yeah, you could say that."

"Did he have anything to do with your getting the job at the station?" she asked.

"Not a thing. It was completely coincidental, but it was good to have a local friend to reconnect with."

"I agree." She thought it was definitely good for Julius to do some male bonding. Perhaps hanging out with a buddy might stop him from flirting with her.

"Have you met his wife, Yasmine?"

"Yes, a couple of times," Mackenzie said, then chewed on a morsel of broccoli. "She seems like a nice person."

"Yeah, she does. I just hope Julius doesn't blow it with this one—wife number three."

"Maybe the third time will be the charm." Mackenzie once wished her first marriage had worked, only because she believed in the whole "till death do you part" vow. But it was not to be and now she was happy to be single. Her new status allowed her to become involved with Ian, someone she clicked with like no one before him.

"They invited us over to dinner," Ian said. "I told them I'd run it by you."

Mackenzie was amazed. That meant Ian had obviously told Julius they were dating. And that certainly wasn't a bad thing in her opinion.

Julius, for all his flirting, had never invited her to his house. Not that she was surprised, since he was married and had no reason to show the place off to a single woman who was unavailable to him.

"I'd love to go with you to dinner at their house."

Ian smiled while sucking on a barbecued rib. "Great! I'll let them know."

Otis came up to the table, wagging his tail. Ian tossed him a bone, but the dog didn't go after it. He just stood there staring at Mackenzie.

She petted him. "Looks like he wants more than just a bone."

Ian moved to her side of the table. "Otis knows good company when he sees it."

"Oh…?" Mackenzie batted her eyes.

"Yeah, just like his owner. Neither of us wants to be very far from you if we can help it."

She flushed. "You're such a charmer."

"I'm an even better kisser," he said.

"Is that so?"

"I'll let you be the judge."

Ian licked his lips and leaned towards her, kissing Mackenzie. She tasted the barbecue sauce and her lips broke into a smile as they kissed.

They stayed in a lip-lock for maybe ten minutes, leaving Mackenzie totally enraptured by the man who had become so much more than a neighbor. He had certainly cast a spell on her and she wasn't ready to be snapped out of it anytime soon.

She forced herself to pull away from his mouth. "I think maybe we should take this inside."

Ian regarded her lustfully. "I couldn't agree more."

He stood and grabbed her hand, stealing another kiss that Mackenzie found impossible to resist.

"What about the leftovers?" she asked. "Shouldn't we put them away?"

"Later. Right now I'd rather focus on satisfying other aspects of our appetite."

Mackenzie's pulse raced at the thought. "Lead the way...."

Ian took pleasure in removing Mackenzie's clothes in his bedroom. As each inch of her soft, bare skin was revealed, he felt more desirous to claim her as his own. Even her smell, a mixture of a flowery fragrance and vanilla, was doing things to him that no other woman had.

His eyes took her in hungrily as she lay waiting on the canopy bed atop a charmeuse sheet. Wishing to experience the entire woman, Ian began with her feet. He massaged them, admiring her long toes that were perfectly manicured with pink-colored nails.

"Mmm…" Mackenzie moaned.

"I'm happy you're enjoying this." He felt good exploring many different levels of sexuality and pleasure with her.

He massaged her legs, which were long and shapely, finding them very appealing. Spreading them, he went for the juncture that lay in between, eager to bring satisfaction to Mackenzie's most private part. He put a finger inside her and felt the thick warm wetness, and it raised the level of his desire to have her. Mackenzie moaned loudly as he stimulated her clitoris, making her even desperate with passion. He could feel Mackenzie shudder wildly.

Mackenzie was ready for Ian and he was equally ready, desperately wanting—needing—to make love to her in that moment. He slipped a condom on and placed her legs on his shoulders before entering her slowly. Her perfect fit, as though made just for him, had Ian hot for sex with her. He threw his head back and squeezed his eyes shut. As Ian made his way deeper inside, the intensity growing stronger, he smiled. All this…and they were just getting started.

Mackenzie was on her knees with Ian behind her as they made love. She could feel him going deeper and deeper inside her, exhilarating all of her senses. His hands gripped her breasts, and his fingers nimbly caressed her nipples, causing currents of electricity to pulsate through her body. She twisted her neck and demanded Ian's lips. He put his tongue in her mouth and Mackenzie got more pleasure as their tongues kissed and tastes mixed. She gripped Ian's buttocks, urging him to go deeper.

Mackenzie had never known such sexual pleasure before. She wasn't sure if the effect would have been the same had they met earlier in life. In the past, she had been reluctant to experiment like this. What was important was that their time was now and she wanted to ride this wave of nonstop ecstasy as long as she could.

Changing positions, Mackenzie swiveled her moist body, wrapping her legs around Ian's waist and her arms around his neck while he remained on his knees. She was certain he was powerful enough to support them both.

Ian did not disappoint. He easily held on to her and drove inside with precision and purpose. Mackenzie wanted to scream, on the verge of another orgasm. She bit into his shoulder, making Ian wince slightly, although, he seemed to immediately shake off the pain.

Both began to feel the throes of climax at once, their breathing coming together in moans and grunts as they slammed into each other with greedy gusto. It was as if they each wanted to soak in every moment of pleasure while they could.

When it was over, they were sweaty and satiated, laughing like lovers who had just run a sexual marathon and had triumphantly reached their goal.

"You never fail to amaze me," Ian said, wiping the perspiration from his head.

"Look who's talking, Mr. Insatiable," returned Mackenzie. Her leg was draped across his.

"Can I help it if you drive me batty with desire?"

"No more than I can." She felt free to be candid about their sexual relationship. Perhaps that came with maturity and finding someone with whom she truly clicked.

"I guess we make a great team," Ian said as he kissed the top of her head.

"In a neighborly sort of way," she teased.

He chuckled. "Yeah, very neighborly. From the moment I saw you, I knew I'd chosen the right house to move into."

Mackenzie was touched by his words, even if they may have been a bit of an exaggeration. But the message was loud and clear—they liked each other.

"I think I've done a good job in welcoming you to the neighborhood." Her voice had the sexual overtones Mackenzie wanted to get across.

Ian grinned. "I would say so."

"You would." She smiled and kissed his chin and then his mouth, her upper lip tickled by his mustache. "Play something for me on the piano."

Ian cocked a brow. "What—you mean now?"

"Yes. I'd like to hear you play." She sensed hesitancy. "I promise not to criticize."

"In that case, I'll give it a shot."

"Thank you." She kissed him, wondering how she'd gotten so lucky to find this man.

Or was it the other way around?

Ian sat on the piano bench, knowing he was pretty rusty. He was also aware that as a singer, Mackenzie may have been expecting something akin to what her regular pianist was capable of. He didn't want to disappoint her or be compared to another. Not after what they had just finished so successfully in bed. There might even be time for another round if things went his way.

Mackenzie sat next to him, while Otis lay lazily on the floor, watching out of curiosity.

"So what are you thinking?" Mackenzie looked at Ian.

He could smell the scent of *them* on her, making him wish they could scrap the piano playing for something much more entertaining.

"Maybe we could do something together," he suggested.

She shook her head. "Oh no. This isn't about me. Besides you'll be at the club tomorrow night and will hear me then."

He frowned. "So I have to be kept in suspense till tomorrow?"

"I'm afraid so."

Ian didn't argue further, knowing her moment was coming soon. This was his chance to leave an impression on her, good or bad. *What should I play for her? What shouldn't I?*

Opting not to read music this time, Ian settled for one of his favorite pieces that he'd mastered once upon a time. "My Romance."

It took him a couple of times to get it right, but in the end Ian felt good playing again for an audience of one, with his loyal dog providing two extra ears. Anything beyond that was still out of his league in this day and age of much more polished and sophisticated piano players than Ian was.

"I love that song," Mackenzie said, humming.

"I thought you might." Ian smiled at her. "Is it part of your act?"

Her eyes twinkled. "As a matter of fact, it is."

Ian could certainly picture Mackenzie crooning the song. "Sure I can't tempt you into singing along with me?"

She considered her response thoughtfully. "Good try, but I'll pass."

Ian continued to play. "Maybe you'll sing it tomorrow."

"Maybe." Mackenzie paused. "All right, yes, I'll do it just for you."

He grinned, wondering if the song would carry as much weight for her as it was beginning to have for him. Spurred on by the thought, Ian tackled another favorite standard that he could handle without messing up too much. "Time after Time."

"Very good," said Mackenzie. "You are definitely a pianist."

"I was one. Now I'm just playing a few notes for a very special lady," Ian told her.

"Well, you can play for me anytime."

Otis barked and Ian chuckled. "Looks like he feels the same."

"There you have it. Use your skills more and you won't lose them altogether," she said with concern.

Ian grinned. "I appreciate the compliment, but for now, my best skills are in other areas."

"Is that so?" Mackenzie tilted her head.

"Yes, it is so." He kissed her neck and felt her react. "I also know just how to put those skills to work."

She closed her eyes as Ian nibbled on her earlobe. "I think you may be right there."

He eyed her romantically and resumed playing the piano, having made his point perfectly.

The next day Mackenzie thought it was time to help Ian grow his own garden. Not to mention a great excuse for them to spend time together doing something she loved.

"Maybe I should just hire you as my gardener and sit back while you work your magic," Ian suggested as they walked into his backyard.

"I don't think so," Mackenzie said. "Not so long as you have two hands, and legs that are workable."

He laughed. "All right, you win."

"No, your backyard is the real winner here. Once it has a real garden, you may be the talk of the neighborhood. You might even want to brag to your listeners about your beautiful garden."

"Good idea," Ian said. "And a clever way to get me in the spirit."

Mackenzie showed her teeth. "Whatever works."

"And just what am I planting?" He eyed the plants she'd set on the picnic table.

"We're keeping it simple, with some red mulberry, blue tulips and toad lilies," she told him.

Ian cocked a brow. "Simple, huh?"

She laughed. "Yes. Once your garden has been established we can try some more sophisticated plants."

"So where do we start?"

"With these." She handed him a pair of work gloves and put on her own. Surveying his healthy green grass, she spotted the perfect section for a garden. "Follow me…"

Within a half hour they had dug up dirt and inserted the plants. Mackenzie let Ian do most of the work so he could get a feel for it.

"Good job," she said. "But the hard part will be maintaining them."

"Can I count on you to help me out here?"

She smiled. "Of course. I'll let you know when you should water."

He grinned crookedly. "Is that all it takes to turn this into a garden like yours?"

"Pretty much. There is one other thing that's very important."

"What's that?"

Mackenzie met his eyes. "I suggest you keep Otis away from the plants. A feisty dog is a surefire way to ruin any garden."

Ian nodded self-consciously. "Got it."

She was sure he would, all things considered. "In that case we're done."

"Not just yet." He moved nearer to her. "A kiss to top things off and I'll be in garden heaven."

Mackenzie laughed, while loving his wit and sexiness. "A kiss it is."

She closed her eyes and puckered lips in anticipation. He didn't disappoint at all in giving a long and tender kiss.

Chapter 11

"I hear you're seeing Ian Kelly," Julius told Mackenzie in her dressing room.

"Yes." She smiled, putting on her earrings.

"Ian and I go back a long way."

"He told me." She tried to imagine the two of them as college pals. Somehow they seemed like an odd couple. Julius was boisterous and Ian was quietly sophisticated. But then opposites do attract.

"Is it serious?" Julius asked curiously.

"We haven't been dating that long," she pointed out. "Right now we're just enjoying each other's company."

"That's cool. It started out that way with me and Yasmine before one thing led to another and, well…" Julius said, lifting his left hand, "she put a ring on my finger and vice versa."

Mackenzie admired the obviously expensive diamond ring. She could only imagine what Yasmine's looked like.

"Nice."

"Yeah, it is." Julius grinned. "Maybe the third time's the charm for me. We'll see."

Mackenzie met his leering eyes and wondered if he was really prepared to do whatever it took to hang on to his marriage. Or would he blow a good thing just as Brent had? And since Ian had been a longtime bachelor, she wondered if he could ever be faithful to one woman. Mackenzie was certain that they were exclusive at least for now. She definitely had no interest in being involved with more than one man at a time. She could only hope that Ian had long gotten out of his system any such need to play the field.

"Did Ian tell you that we'd like to have the two of you over for dinner?"

"Yes, he mentioned it," she said. "It sounds like fun."

"Yasmine's into that type of thing." Julius checked his BlackBerry handheld. "How about next Wednesday?"

Mackenzie mentally studied her own schedule. "If it works for Ian, count me in."

He nodded to the done deal. "Well, I'd better let you get ready for tonight."

"Thank you."

"By the way, Dorian's a little under the weather."

She widened her eyes. "But he's here, right?" The thought of her pianist being a no-show scared Mackenzie. She had worked with only one other piano man and the results had been nearly disastrous.

"You know Dorian. You'd have to practically tie him down to keep him away from work." Julius put a stick of gum in his mouth. "Just keep the arrangements simple and I'm sure no one will be the wiser."

She breathed a sigh of relief. "Will do."

"I understand Ian will be here tonight."

"Yes."

"Good. I'm sure he'll get a real treat, assuming you haven't already given him a private performance."

"I haven't." *At least, not in the vocal arena.*

Julius smiled. "Then bring the house down in honor of my main man being in town."

As if I don't already have enough pressure. "I'll see what I can do about that."

Mackenzie would be the first to admit that Dorian wasn't looking too good. But it was how he felt inside that counted the most. Wasn't it?

"Are you sure you're up to this?" she questioned, concerned for his health above everything else.

He sniffled, wiping his nose with a tissue. "Yeah, I'll be fine. It's the flu bug going around. For some reason it went after me and caught me when my immune system was down. It's nothin' that the next few days off won't cure. I've got enough juice in the engine to get it done tonight, as long as that jazzy voice of yours can carry us through."

Mackenzie took him at this word. Still, she heeded Julius's advice and decided they would stick with songs that weren't too complicated for her pianist.

"I'm sure I can hold my own."

He smiled weakly from one side of his mouth. "That's my gal."

"So let's put on a show!" she told him.

"Ready when you are." He sighed. "Go get 'em!"

Mackenzie had chosen a periwinkle gown and matching suede T-straps for this special performance. Her hair was in a sophisticated updo and she wore a teardrop dangle necklace.

She spotted Ian in a front-row seat sitting with Julius and Yasmine. They were laughing and chatting while waiting for the evening's headlining performance. As she took her spot, Mackenzie hoped she didn't disappoint.

"Welcome, everyone," she said glowingly. "I'm so happy you could come tonight. Please give a hand to my fabulous pianist, Dorian Javier."

The audience responded accordingly and Dorian stood and gave a bow.

"We're going to get started with a terrific song that such jazz greats as Billie Holiday sang so hauntingly," Mackenzie said. "It's called 'Lover Man.'"

She planted her eyes on Ian thoughtfully. He lifted his drink to her, eliciting a smile from her even as she tried to keep the nerves under control.

You're my lover man and I couldn't have found a better one.

She looked to Dorian for his cue and he flashed her a thumbs-up. Turning to the audience, Mackenzie swallowed, gathered herself and began singing as the words ran across the screen in her head.

It didn't take long for Mackenzie to get warmed up and caught in the moment. She sang with her heart and soul, actually feeling herself grow stronger with each passing minute. She was sure that Ian had something to do with that. He inspired her through his presence and support to make certain it was a performance to remember.

"Thank you so much," she said gleefully after the first song as the applause was deafening. *Now the pressure's really on.* She was ready to meet the challenge.

Mackenzie took a breath and gazed at Ian. He gave her an approving nod. She showed her teeth in appreciation, believing she had already won him over in song and romance. It boded well for the future.

"This next song is every bit as moving," she told the audience and Ian in particular. "It's called, 'But Beautiful.'"

Mackenzie sang it as though written for her; a burst of adrenaline kept her voice sexy and resonant. She gave it her all and got as much in return. Performing in front of Ian for the first time couldn't have gone better. She had pulled it off and could now relax as she went through the rest of her routine.

"She's terrific, isn't she?" Julius asked in awe as he faced Ian.

"Absolutely." He was in complete agreement. Ian could barely take his eyes off Mackenzie, who looked as great as she sounded. Apart from a voice reminiscent of Sarah Vaughan and Shirley Horn, she could also work the audience with the soft swaying of her hips and luminescent smile.

Ian imagined Mackenzie could sing anywhere if she wanted to. She was that good. He also knew that to make it in this business as a professional, one's heart and soul had to be in it full-time. He didn't get the impression Mackenzie was ready to pursue singing as a career, believing she was more comfortable with it as a part-time gig.

Ian watched her, mesmerized. For his part, he'd certainly be willing to help her as a singer any way he could, including airtime on his morning show. He had no doubt his listeners would be quickly hooked on Mackenzie and her talent. Just as he was, over and beyond her strengths as a beautiful and very sexy businesswoman and romantic lady.

"Now you see why I want to hang on to her," Julius said genuinely.

Ian smiled and thought how good it felt to truly hold on to Mackenzie. "Of course." *If I could I'd never let her go.*

Julius chuckled. "Can you imagine how far we could have gone had she been part of our band back in the day?"

"Not sure I want to hear this." Yasmine whispered as she rolled her eyes.

Ian grinned. "It would have been strictly professional," he promised.

"Uh-huh," she said with misgivings.

"He's right," Julius insisted. "Mackenzie would have been dynamic to an up-and-coming young band trying to make ends meet, but you're the one I really wish I'd met years ago."

She blushed, kissing him.

Ian let them do their thing while refocusing on the lady of the night. The thought of having gotten to know Mackenzie earlier in life appealed to him. Who knows how far they would have come. He was sure they would have brought out the best in one another. At least they were able to meet and bond at this time when both were available and looking for someone who complemented the other.

Mackenzie sang three more numbers, each with her signature style, and with the enthusiastic appreciation of the audience. When she and Dorian went on break before the second session, Ian snuck into her dressing room.

"Hey, lovely lady."

"Hi." She hugged him, and Ian inhaled her fruity perfume.

He kissed her cheek, not wanting to mess up her lipstick. "You've been holding back on me."

Her lashes curled. "Have I?"

"Yes. I didn't realize just what a dynamic stage performer you were."

She flashed a radiant smile. "All you had to do was ask."

"Why didn't I think of that?" Ian grinned playfully. "I can see now why you didn't want to sing when I was playing the piano. I would have tarnished that beautiful voice, no doubt."

"I don't think so," she said. "I just wanted to keep it a surprise until you heard it on stage for the first time."

"Well, it was definitely worth the wait." He paused. "I'd say this is your calling."

"You really think so?"

"I know so. There aren't many singers who can bring it home like you."

She blushed. "Flattery just might get you everywhere."

He felt a twinge of arousal. "I'm counting on that."

"So am I."

They were interrupted when Julius came in. He had a dour look on his face.

"We've got a problem," he said.

Mackenzie raised her chin. "What?"

"Dorian just threw up in his dressing room. The man's running a high fever and is really out of it."

She frowned. "I didn't realize he was that ill. Especially since he told me he'd be able to get through the evening."

"Maybe he convinced himself of that." Julius pursed his lips. "But bottom line is he's not going to be able to go on for the last set."

"That's too bad," Ian said. He'd really looked forward to more jazz vocals from Mackenzie's lips.

Mackenzie sighed. "So we're done for today?"

"Not necessarily." Julius's voice had a catch to it. "Did you hear that crowd out there? They'll go nuts if the performance is cut short after what you gave them for starters."

"So what are you suggesting?" she asked uneasily.

Julius turned to Ian. "I'm saying you can fill in for Dorian."

Ian's brow furrowed. "What?"

"I know it's asking a lot, old buddy, but it's only for one set. We both know you can do it."

"No, we don't." Ian met Mackenzie's gaze, then Julius's. "I haven't played professionally in years."

"So what? It shouldn't be that difficult to get it going again, especially if you avoid any complex numbers."

"I don't know about this." The last thing Ian wanted was

to make a fool of himself, even at a club where he wasn't known. On the other hand, as a deejay for a jazz station, this might be something fun for his audience.

"You two have chemistry," insisted Julius. "I can see that. Why not put it to good use as a one-night-only affair before an audience?"

Mackenzie looked up at Ian. "I'm willing to give it a try, if you are."

"Are you sure about this?"

"Why not? I've heard you play. I think we can make it work."

"What about practicing together?"

She applied some powder to her face. "I guess we'll just have to wing it and hope for the best."

"So what do you say?" Julius pressed. "Are you in?"

Given that they were both on board, Ian couldn't refuse. "I'm in," he told them reluctantly.

"Great. I'll keep the audience warm while you two find three or four songs you feel confident about. We'll all keep our fingers crossed that you can pull it off."

And what if they didn't? Although Ian wondered if this could impact their personal relationship, he smiled at Mackenzie. "So where do we start?"

Mackenzie had no idea if it would work, but was more than willing to try. Clicking musically usually took practice. She and Ian had not had any—not including their impromptu session at his house, where he had done all the work while she admired him.

Yet there was no denying the chemistry between them in other areas. So why couldn't it work here, too, if only for a onetime performance? Stranger things had happened. They just might bring down the house.

The alternative was not an option. She certainly didn't

want to disappoint her fans by canceling the second session, even if many would surely understand that sometimes stuff happened. It was no one's fault that Dorian was ill and unable to carry on.

It was great that Ian was willing to take a crack at it and give it his all to fill in for Dorian. This made Mackenzie appreciate having him in her life all the more—even if things didn't work out.

In the meantime, she was worried about her regular pianist and hoped that his illness didn't linger.

Mackenzie gazed at Ian, who had made himself comfortable at the piano. Ian was resplendent in a gray herringbone sport coat over a silk-blend black shirt and ivory pleated slacks.

"Are you ready?" she whispered, feeling the butterflies.

Ian flashed a confident smile. "Let's put on a show the folks won't soon forget!"

Mackenzie's eyes crinkled and she readied herself on stage. "Hello, everybody," she said sweetly. "Thank you for sticking around. You may or may not have noticed that my regular piano man is no longer in his familiar spot. Unfortunately Dorian has fallen prey to the flu bug, which I'm sure some of you can relate to." She sighed. "The good news is that we have a stand-in pianist who should be able to get the job done without missing a beat. I'd like to introduce you to Ian Kelly. If the name sounds at all familiar, it just may be because he's the host of a very popular jazz show on Cheri Village's own KRDQ. Won't you give him a warm welcome."

The audience cheered wildly, and Ian seemed slightly taken aback as he stood and gave a bow, before blowing kisses. The last one was directed at Mackenzie, landing right on her lips, she imagined.

She beamed and went over in her mind the songs they would tackle. They had agreed to do four songs that Ian had a good handle on. "We're going to get started with a classic by any standard, no pun intended. It's called, 'They Can't Take That Away From Me.'"

Mackenzie made eye contact with Ian as her pulse raced with nervous tension. On cue he began playing and she moved right into her powerful vocals to the song. Though she detected a couple of missteps in their coordination, Mackenzie doubted the audience noticed in any way. Soon they were in good rhythm and she gained confidence. She and Ian could actually pull this off as though paired together for years.

Indeed, Mackenzie believed that with continued practice they could probably make a dynamic musical team that could woo jazz fans all around. As it was, she had no immediate plans to take her show on the road and Ian seemed content as a radio personality.

Overall she preferred to focus on their personal growth as a couple and not try to be too many things to each other. Mackenzie was sure Ian was of the same mind.

After singing two classics, "Harlem Nocturne" and "I've Got the World on a String," they finished with a stirring rendition of "My Romance."

Mackenzie gave it her all and could see that Ian seemed to put a little extra into it, too, as though the song had been written for them. She wondered if they both felt the words spoke for them and their own destiny even while enjoying each other one day at a time.

The audience was clearly moved by the performance and gave them a standing ovation. Ian stood alongside Mackenzie. They held hands and bowed.

Then, as if this had been part of the plan all along, he gave her a soul-stirring kiss, to the audience's—and Mackenzie's—utter delight.

* * *

When they got back to her house, Mackenzie wasted no time going after Ian's inviting lips, wanting to complete the slow seduction that had begun with their romantic musical performance at the lounge.

She was aroused by thoughts of Ian's virtuosity and dizzy from the musk of his cologne.

"I want you inside me," she demanded in a voice of desperation.

Ian sighed in her mouth. "You're singing to the piano man," he uttered huskily. "We're both totally in tune on that score."

"Say no more." Mackenzie led Ian to the bedroom and pushed him down on the bed with anticipation. She grabbed the condom he'd placed on the nightstand, and slid it onto him. Climbing atop his naked body, she put him inside her and immediately contracted around him before gliding slowly up and down.

She pushed her breasts in Ian's face, making him suck her nipples. Moaning loudly, Mackenzie felt her heart pounding relentlessly as they made love with a passion that had grown with each intimate act. Ian grunted while gripping her buttocks and meeting Mackenzie halfway with each thrust. She pressed her open mouth to his and they kissed with utter devotion, filled with the need to conquer their desires once again. A primordial sound came from Mackenzie's mouth as a potent wave of pleasure engulfed her. She constricted around Ian, capturing his moan in her mouth as they climaxed together. The bed shook around them for a full five minutes as they rode the wave of ecstasy and frenetic lovemaking to its shuddering conclusion.

"Guess we may need to play sweet music together more often," Ian said, catching his breath.

"I think we've already proven we're in sync," Mackenzie countered boldly, still atop him, back arched.

"Good point."

"I thought you would agree."

"So now we're reading each other's thoughts?"

"Got a problem with that?"

"None whatsoever." He ran a hand across her chest. "Come to think of it, the only problem I'm having these days is when we're apart."

She ran a hand across the side of his face and gently said, "Guess we'll have to try not to be apart too often."

"Sounds like a good plan." He gripped her waist. "Now come down here and give me a kiss."

"Your wish is my command."

Mackenzie collapsed onto Ian and found his waiting lips, meeting his tongue with hers. She tried to remember when she had felt so sexually open and been so satisfied. She realized she never had. Not with her college boyfriend. Or her husband. Only Ian had been able to bring out such wanton desire and give her such fire-quenching satisfaction.

Mackenzie realized what her heart had probably been trying to tell her from the very beginning of this connection with Ian. What she was feeling for this man went well beyond sexual fulfillment. He was starting to affect her very being, to cause her heart to palpitate every time she thought of him. This feeling intensified whenever she was around him, and whenever he touched her. Mackenzie was starting to fall in love with Ian Kelly.

Chapter 12

"Good morning, folks," Ian said into the microphone at the station on Monday. "I don't know how many of you happened to be at the Deer Lounge in Burlington on Saturday night—probably not too many of you—but, if you weren't there, you missed quite a show. Your very own deejay sat in on the piano when the regular piano man began to feel a bit under the weather.

"I won't bore you with the details, other than to say that I happened to be in the right place at the right time and I had a blast. If any of you caught my performance, then by all means, phone in and let me and everyone else know how I did. Just be kind to someone who's not thinking about quitting his day job in the foreseeable future.

"And for everyone who wasn't there, you should know I played for a very talented lounge singer named Mackenzie Reese. If you want to hear Sarah Vaughan and Ella Fitzgerald all wrapped up in one, with a bit of Billie Holiday and Shirley

Horn thrown in for good measure, you can catch Ms. Reese there every other Saturday night. I highly recommend her performance.

"And I hope you get over the flu soon, Dorian," Ian added. During his little monologue, Ian thought of a song to play while thinking of Mackenzie and her many talents. Before beginning the song, Ian said, "Hey, Ms. Jazzy Vocalist, if you're hearing me this morning, this one's for you."

He played Roberta Flack's version of what had quickly become their song, "My Romance."

"Someone's certainly in a good mood," Doug said.

Ian could hear Doug through his headphones and see him through the window of his cubicle where he would be giving the news shortly.

"I'm always in a good mood," Ian said.

"How about extra good then?"

Guess I can't pretend to not feel as good as I do. "All right you got me. I'm feeling pretty damn good right now."

"Does it have anything to do with that gardener neighbor?" Doug asked. "Or is it the jazz singer who has you feeling all giddy?"

"Actually they're one and the same," Ian was proud to say. "And yes, she has everything to do with it."

"So, you are taking neighborly love to a whole new level then?"

"Maybe I am."

Ian chewed on that thought. *Neighborly love?* Had what he was feeling for Mackenzie reached that point?

Yes, he had been in love before, but it usually ran out of steam at about the same time the woman got too serious too soon, sending him flying in the opposite direction. But things were different with Mackenzie. She was not the type of woman he could imagine running away from. They seemed to be kindred spirits on too many levels to let her slip away. The fact that Mackenzie's son was living with her ex on the opposite side of the country meant that she and Ian could spend more time enjoying each other without complications.

But what about love? Was she willing to put herself out there emotionally after a failed marriage? It occurred to Ian that maybe it was too soon to think in such affectionate terms with his next-door neighbor. Things were going great between them.

Better not to rock the boat by bringing love into the equation right now, he thought. *But I can't help the way the sweet and sexy lady makes me feel, especially when I haven't felt like this about anyone before.*

Ian held on to that thought while listening to Doug report the latest news.

"I wish I'd caught that dual performance," Sophia said to Mackenzie as they worked on their respective clients. Both had heard Ian talking about it on the radio before Mackenzie could share the news herself.

"So do I," she admitted as she finished curling her client's hair. "You would've loved it."

"I'm sure of that," Sophia said as she trimmed her client. "Does that mean you're dumping your current piano player for your sexy boyfriend?"

"Just tilt your head a little to the right," Mackenzie told her client and then looked over at Sophia. "Hardly. Ian and I agree that ours was a onetime thing in the public arena. Dorian will still play for me at the club."

She surmised that Julius might have a different opinion, given his ties to Ian and the impression Ian had left on him Saturday night. But it was highly doubtful Julius could or would pay Ian enough to pry him away from what he had to be making as a popular radio deejay. Besides, Dorian had been a loyal employee since the lounge opened and had a good working relationship with the other singers as well as Mackenzie. She saw no reason to upend that arrangement to enter into an uncertain musical partnership with the man she was romantically involved with.

"Maybe your man can introduce me to someone," said Freda, another one of the hairdressers.

Mackenzie gave her wide-eyed look. "I thought you were with that baker?"

"Was," she said sourly. "Seems he forgot we were supposed to be dating. He hasn't called me in two weeks."

"I'd say that's your cue to move on."

"I'm trying to, but I could use a little help from my friends."

Mackenzie felt for her, having gone down that road herself with men who turned out to be no good.

"I can always ask Ian if he knows any single men." She doubted that was the case from what he'd already told her, but it couldn't hurt to inquire. She mused that perhaps Sophia could part with one of the men she kept on a string.

"Speaking of…" Sophia said, shifting her gaze toward the entry.

Mackenzie looked in the direction of the front door and saw Ian walk in.

He grinned broadly. "Hi, ladies. I could use a head shave and buff."

"You've come to the right place," Mackenzie promised, her heart skipping a beat at the sight of Ian in her hair salon.

Ian was introduced to the employees and engaged in small talk with Sophia. But his focus was mainly on Mackenzie. He'd been thinking about her all day and finally took the time to come to her workplace to have his head done professionally. He was used to shaving it himself. Now that he'd begun dating a hairstylist, Ian wanted to pass some business her way.

He waited patiently until Mackenzie had finished with her client—not wanting anyone else working on him—before taking a seat at her station.

"I've been waiting to get you in this chair," she whispered sexily in his ear. "I was beginning to think you'd lost your nerve."

He chuckled uneasily, getting a whiff of her honeysuckle fragrance.

"I have nerves of steel," he said evenly.

"Oh, really?" She pulled the chair back. "We'll see about that."

"Be gentle now," Ian joked a little nervously as Mackenzie lathered his head.

"Aren't I always?" she teased.

"No complaints thus far." He thought about their lovemaking. It was not always so gentle, but it was very effective and invariably left them both still hungry for more.

"In that case, just relax and let me pamper you," Mackenzie said sweetly.

Ian liked the sound of that. "Please do—all you want." He could well imagine spending a lifetime being pampered by her and doing the same in return.

Mackenzie shaved his head while Ian lay back dreamily. "So how do you like our place?" she asked.

"I like it," he said, noting that all the other chairs were filled. "Looks like you've got a thriving business going here." This didn't surprise him at all. Obviously she had a head for business and knowledge of this industry, making it work for her.

"Well, it's not always this crowded, but we do all right."

"We can always use a little extra publicity," Sophia shouted across several chairs. "Don't let us stop you from giving Magnificent Hair Salon a plug on your radio show, Mr. Deejay."

"She didn't just say that," Mackenzie whispered, clearly embarrassed.

Ian smiled, taking it in stride. "Consider it done," he said easily, wishing he'd thought to do this sooner. After all, what good was it being a radio personality if he couldn't use the platform on occasion for promoting the right things? In this instance, he saw it as a fringe benefit of dating a sexy hairstylist. "I'd be happy to plug the salon and even send some of my colleagues your way."

"Thank you for being Mackenzie's man," Sophia said. "Don't know what any of us would ever do without you."

Everyone laughed, including Ian. "Hopefully you'll never have to find out," he kidded, then turned serious. "I don't intend to let Mackenzie get away, so I'm afraid you'll have to get used to my hanging around."

"You are so sweet," Mackenzie said, drying his head. "And also good to go. But you'll get no complaints out of me or apparently anyone else if you choose to stay."

Ian grinned, enjoying the repartee and camaraderie there. Most of all, he loved spending time with Mackenzie in another one of her elements.

"That just may be the best idea I've heard all day," he told her good-naturedly.

Chapter 13

"I want to come home!"

Mackenzie listened with shock to her son's words over the phone that evening. She stopped watering her indoor plants. "You what?"

"I'm tired of being out here," Ryan complained.

I'm not tired of enjoying the freedom you've given me by living with your father. But if it comes with a price that's too high, I'd much rather have you home.

"What happened?" Mackenzie's voice was full of concern. "What's making you feel this way all of a sudden?"

Ryan was mute.

"You told me you were happy living in L.A.," she noted. Had he been telling the truth?

"I was," he claimed.

"So what changed?"

He paused. "It's just gotten old."

"You'll have to do better than that." Mackenzie sighed. "You can't just change your mind out of the blue."

"I don't belong here." Ryan snorted.

Mackenzie's brow creased. "Says who? Your stepmother? Dad?"

"No one."

She refused to believe there wasn't something behind this change of heart. If not Deborah or Brent, then who? *Calm down, at least till you can get to the bottom of this.*

"Did you get into a fight?"

Ryan coughed. "Yeah, once, but that has nothing to do with my decision."

Mackenzie fumed that he'd gotten into trouble and Brent hadn't bothered to tell her about it. Or apparently try to prevent it from happening in the first place. *Was that his way to toughen up Ryan—by encouraging him to fight?* They could talk about that later.

"Well, is it a girl?" Mackenzie was well aware Ryan was old enough to notice girls and vice versa. He had already indicated as much. Had he set his sights on someone, only to be rejected?

"No, it's not a girl," he insisted testily. "It's just me, okay?"

"No, it's not okay!" Mackenzie raised her voice, though she hadn't meant to. But she didn't seem to be getting very far with him. "There's obviously something you aren't telling me. One moment you say that California is the coolest place on the planet and now you're ready to give all that up and come home. I'm not buying it. Not without a reasonable explanation."

"You're saying I can't come home?" Ryan asked sharply.

Mackenzie gritted her teeth. Everything was going so well in her life. Business was great. She was in a fabulous relationship with her ultrasexy next-door neighbor. Things could not be going any better.

Now her teenage son, who had left of his own accord, wanted to turn her life upside down by returning home without revealing what was behind it.

The mother in Mackenzie knew she could never reject her son at the end of the day, no matter his reasons or if it meant interfering with her life and freedom. She loved Ryan too much for that, even if his dad may not have been able to say the same.

But what about Ian? Surely he would understand that her child's health and well-being had to come first over everything? Hadn't she made that perfectly clear?

Then Mackenzie thought about Ryan's eagerness to leave home, believing life without her looking over his shoulder all the time would be better. She hadn't necessarily been in agreement with him at the time, but let him have his way. Now she wondered if that had been such a good idea. Or maybe it had been a great one that Ryan needed to own up to. Hadn't he reached the age where he needed to shoulder some responsibility for his actions and not put the onus back on her?

"What does your father have to say about this?" she asked, sitting down.

"I don't care what he has to say," Ryan returned.

Mackenzie would not leave it at that. "Well, I do! You cannot make this decision on your own without consulting with him and your stepmom."

"Why can't you just let me come home?" Ryan's voice deepened.

"Because you *are* home!" Mackenzie decided she had to remain firm about this and not let him walk all over her. Otherwise she might always be subject to his whims. "You chose to go live with your dad—you actually insisted. Now you've gotten your wish, and I won't let you do a flip-flop now simply because you've had a bad week."

"You don't understand."

"Maybe I would if you explained it to me better," she said, softening her tone.

Again he let silence speak for him.

Mackenzie drew a breath. "Whatever problems you're having, you have to talk to your father about them. That's what he's there for. They won't disappear simply by running away from them, and it's not being very fair to me."

"Just forget it!" Ryan grumbled.

"No, let's not forget it," Mackenzie argued. "Talk to me, Ryan. I've always made myself available to you. All I ask in return is that you be straight with me."

"How can I when you won't trust me enough not to ask so many questions?" he said unevenly.

"That doesn't make any sense."

"Sorry I bothered you," Ryan tossed out.

The phone call abruptly ended.

Mackenzie couldn't believe he'd hung up on her. How dare he do such a thing without cause? Or was she too insistent for answers that he simply shut off? She felt a little guilty, as though she were turning her back on him. Deep down Mackenzie realized that making him grow up and face his issues was the best thing she could do for her son, even if he didn't see it that way right now.

So why do I wish I could just take him in my arms and tell him that everything will be all right?

She called Brent, not feeling she should have to deal with this all by herself.

It was Deborah who answered his cell phone.

"Mackenzie…" she said guardedly.

Mackenzie bit her lip at having to speak with her ex's new wife. Both had gone out of their way to avoid this whenever possible. "Hi. I'm calling to talk to Brent. Is he there?"

"He's in the shower right now. Sorry."

So was Mackenzie. Seemed as if whenever she needed him on behalf of their son, Brent was always occupied. Was that a bad sign?

"I can have him call you back, if you like," Deborah suggested tonelessly.

Mackenzie stiffened. "Yes, please tell him to call me as soon as he can."

"Is something wrong?"

Mackenzie's first instinct was to keep this between her and Brent, seeing that Ryan was their responsibility. But as Deborah was now his wife and a part of Ryan's life, there was no reason to shut her out. Especially since she might be the root cause of the problem.

"I just spoke with Ryan," Mackenzie began. "He wants to move back to Vermont."

"Oh, really?"

"I wouldn't say this if it weren't true," Mackenzie said flatly.

"This is the first I've heard of it," Deborah claimed.

Mackenzie was skeptical. "Ryan says he doesn't like living there anymore. Maybe you can tell me what's going on?"

She waited a moment. "If you really want to know what's going on, I'll tell you. Your son doesn't respect me and barely respects his father."

"What…?" Mackenzie felt her temperature rise.

"He expects us to wait on him hand and foot while feeling that *no* rules should apply to him."

"I can't believe that," Mackenzie stated. She hadn't raised him that way. Could a few months have made that big a difference?

"Can't or won't?" Deborah challenged her.

Mackenzie's nostrils flared. She didn't like Deborah, of all people, questioning Ryan's character. But Mackenzie recognized that during an adjustment period any teenager might need some time to deal with the changes in life. Apparently Deborah didn't understand this.

"Ryan's a good boy," she said lamely.

"Never said he wasn't," Deborah countered. "Doesn't change the facts any that he's developed a major attitude and we can't seem to reach him."

Mackenzie refrained from attacking Deborah's parenting skills, though she suspected that she was a major part of the reason Ryan wasn't happy.

"Look, Ryan wanted to go live with his father, and Brent and I agreed it was a good idea. I expect you to do what you can to try and make this work."

Deborah gave a wry chuckle. "I'm not a miracle worker!"

"And I'm not asking you to be," Mackenzie countered sharply. "Just a good stepmother. Someone who has his back when times get tough."

"Maybe he'd prefer that *you* had his back instead of dumping him off on us," Deborah responded. "Isn't that what this is all about?"

"I have my son's back, thank you." Mackenzie sucked in a deep breath of vexation. "And no, it's not what this is all about. My son deserves to be loved and feel at home."

"So let him be loved and at home with you!"

"I don't recall forcing Ryan on you and his father," Mackenzie pointed out.

"Call it anything you want," Deborah said. "Clearly it was a mistake for him to have come out here."

"Is that how Brent feels, too?" Mackenzie asked point-blank.

Deborah paused. "Maybe you should ask him."

"Maybe I will," Mackenzie snapped.

"Whatever. I'll tell Brent you called."

When Mackenzie hung up, she was furious. Had Ryan been made to feel like a stranger in his father's home? With his stepmother the culprit? Or was Deborah just venting when the opportunity came as a means to free Brent from his responsibility as a parent?

Mackenzie intended to get to the bottom of it. She only wanted what was best for Ryan, even if he didn't seem to have a clue. At the moment, she sincerely believed it was staying right where he was. Otherwise he would never learn how to deal with adversity, which surely would not end in his life at fifteen.

Mackenzie turned her thoughts to Brent, who seemed derelict in his responsibility. She was still not quite sure if his new wife spoke for him, or out of frustration. Or perhaps cruelty.

She wouldn't allow him to skirt being a father simply because he had a new wife. Ryan came with the package the moment Deborah had decided to marry Brent, whether she liked it or not.

Mackenzie hated that Ryan had to be part of a broken home, having never wanted him to have to deal with the inevitable consequences of a failed marriage. But that was real life in today's times. Ryan had to learn that no matter his circumstances, he couldn't play Ping-Pong with his parents whenever he felt like it.

She hoped Brent backed her up on this and acted accordingly to help his son make the necessary adjustments to his life in California.

Mackenzie had no idea how any of this might impact her relationship with Ian. Maybe there would be no effect. Or maybe it would change everything, irrespective of her strong feelings for the man.

Chapter 14

On Wednesday Mackenzie rode with Ian to Julius's home for dinner. She was looking forward to seeing the lakefront property she'd heard so much about and felt it would be a good opportunity to get to know Yasmine better.

Mackenzie's concern about Ryan threatened to put a damper on the evening. She hadn't heard anything from Brent for the past two days other than to say, "I'll look into it and get back to you." *So why haven't you gotten back to me?* she wondered over and over again.

Mackenzie feared that Brent might be unduly influenced by Deborah and end up turning his back on Ryan. She didn't want to even think about how this could affect her son.

"Are you okay over there?" Ian's deep voice intruded upon her thoughts.

Mackenzie sighed. She had spoken only vaguely about Ryan's situation, not wanting to scare Ian off at the prospect of dating a woman who suddenly had a teenage son living at home. He hadn't signed up for that, and Mackenzie wasn't ready to broach the subject with him yet.

Her eyes crinkled. "I'm fine," she told him and rested her hand on his knee. "I just hope I'm not dressed too casually."

Ian assessed Mackenzie up and down and seemed to be more than pleased with what he saw.

"Not at all. You look great."

"Thank you," she said as she gazed over at him and felt amazed at just how handsome he was. "Ditto."

Ian flashed his teeth. "We do make quite a pair."

She needed to know. "You really think so?"

"Of course. Don't you?"

"Yes." Mackenzie was beginning to feel that way more than ever. She just didn't want to see their fairy-tale romance fall by the wayside due to circumstances beyond her control. But the fact remained that, whether near or far, Ryan was a part of her life and always would be.

Can Ian live with that?

Ian knew Mackenzie was worried about her son. She had mentioned something about him being unhappy living with his father, while stressing that the status quo was unlikely to change anytime soon.

What does that mean? Ian couldn't help asking himself. *Could he actually return to live with her somewhere down the line?*

Ian liked things the way they were and wasn't particularly keen on seeing their easy relationship threatened by Mackenzie's teenage son and the baggage and drama he would likely bring back with him. Since it was out of his hands, Ian wouldn't make waves unnecessarily. He could only hope for the best and not look for trouble where there was none at the moment. He cared for Mackenzie too much to think about rain clouds marring their otherwise sunny relationship.

When they arrived at the house, Julius and Yasmine greeted them.

"Welcome to our home." Yasmine gave Mackenzie a hug.

"Thanks for inviting me."

"Hey, you're like family the way Julius talks about you."

"I only speak the truth," he said flatly. "The lady is gorgeous and she knows how to sing jazz."

"Listen to your husband," Ian chimed in. "I happen to agree with him every step of the way."

"Stop it, you two." Mackenzie colored. "I'm not here to perform, okay?"

Yasmine took her arm. "Don't worry about them. There will be no singing tonight, just a nice quiet dinner with friends."

"I can live with that," Ian said, happy to be able to socialize with Mackenzie.

He wanted them both to get to know each other's friends as part of the larger circle of their relationship, which had grown by leaps and bounds.

As far as he was concerned there was plenty of upside yet to be discovered.

Mackenzie was given the grand tour, and she liked what she saw. The architecture was amazing with its custom woodwork and inlaid bamboo flooring. There were double French doors and marble fireplaces in multiple rooms, with dimmers throughout featuring art deco sconces.

"Hope you're both famished," Julius said, leading them to the formal dining room. "When Yasmine cooks, she sometimes doesn't know when to stop."

Ian laughed. "I can probably eat enough for the two of us if Mackenzie prefers to keep her beautiful figure."

"I think you mean that you'd rather she kept it." Julius grinned mischievously.

Yasmine took Mackenzie's hand. "Men! They always want us to keep our weight down, but they encourage us to cook their favorite dishes. It's totally unfair."

Mackenzie smiled. "You're right. But we're entitled to enjoy our food every now and then just as they do."

Half an hour later they were seated at a solid wood square table eating a dinner of pork roast, asparagus, red potatoes, dinner rolls and caramelized pears and walnuts. A nice local red wine completed the meal.

"This is just too delicious!" Mackenzie used a cloth napkin to wipe the corners of her mouth.

"Thank you." Yasmine smiled. "I love to cook. I consider it a gift that my mother passed down to me and my sister."

"She taught you well," Ian said as he savored a piece of the roast.

"I tell her that all the time," said Julius, before eating a mouthful of potatoes. "But I think she just takes it for granted."

Yasmine chuckled. "As long as I can keep you coming back for more, then I'm happy."

"You keep cooking it and I'll keep eating it, baby," he promised.

Mackenzie pondered the fact that although Julius was on his third wife he and Yasmine seemed so happy together. Maybe he'd realized it was time to settle down once and for all. She wondered if Ian might be beginning to think in those terms. Or was marriage something that might never be in the cards for him?

Do I even want to walk down the aisle again after being burned once?

Her heart told Mackenzie yes, assuming the feeling was mutual, no matter what obstacles might lie ahead.

"How's Dorian doing?" Ian asked.

"He's recovering nicely," Julius told him. "It's hard to keep a good man down."

"Good to hear."

"Of course, if we're ever in need of someone to fill in for emergencies, I think we know who to call now."

Ian chuckled. "Not so fast. My listeners were quick to remind me that I should quit while I'm ahead. And I just might heed their advice." He met Mackenzie's eyes. "But the memories from our performance will last forever."

"That's so sweet." She blushed, wishing she could kiss him right then and there, and knowing she would have if they had not been seated on opposite sides of the table. "We can always team up again at your house when that baby grand needs someone to warm it up."

Ian lifted his glass. "Sounds good to me."

"Spoken like two people who truly care about each other," Yasmine offered.

Julius hoisted his wine glass. "I'll drink to that."

She beamed. "Yes, let's."

"Make that three," Ian said.

All eyes turned to Mackenzie. Since she definitely cared very much about Ian and was sure he pretty much shared those feelings, she was only too happy to join the toast.

"Four sounds even better!" Mackenzie raised her glass enthusiastically.

"Don't tell me the love bug has bitten you, too?" Julius stood on the opposite side of his pool table watching Ian chalk his cue stick.

He arched a brow. *Have I given myself away so easily?* "What makes you think that?"

"Come on, man! You couldn't take your eyes off her."

"Can you blame me?"

"Not one bit." Julius took aim at a ball. "In fact, to tell you the truth, if I weren't a married man and all, I might've gone after her myself."

Ian's jaw tightened at the notion. "Guess I'm lucky you are happily wed."

Knowing Julius, Ian had no doubt he'd made a pass at Mackenzie at one time or another. He was also equally certain the effort failed. While she was an unattached lady before he came into the picture, Ian didn't believe for one moment that Mackenzie would go after a married man. She had more integrity than that. Not to mention that she had been on the receiving end of an unfaithful marriage. She would never do that to Yasmine. Ian wasn't sure the same could be said for Julius, considering his marital track record.

"How about you?" Julius stared at him. "When are you going to let Mackenzie—or some other woman—make an honest man out of you?"

Ian pondered the question. Most of his relationships with women had practically ended before they ever started. Marriage for him seemed like something that would never happen. But that was before he met Mackenzie. The way she made his blood run hot as no woman had previously told Ian she was someone he could definitely see himself marrying. Spending the night with Mackenzie in a honeymoon suite on some tropical paradise island excited Ian more than he could say. But there were still practical matters that couldn't be ignored.

For one, was Mackenzie even interested in going down the marriage aisle a second time? Or was she comfortable with things between them just as they were? And was Ian ready to become a stepfather, even if the stepson was nearly three thousand miles away?

Ian met his friend's gaze. "I can't answer that right now."

"Can't or won't?"

Ian grinned. "Let me put it to you this way. I think I've found the woman I'd like to give a ring to and spend the rest of my life with."

"Thought so." Julius moved to the end of the table for a better shot. "Something tells me she wouldn't hesitate if you put it out there for her."

"You think?"

"Don't you?"

Ian sighed while measuring up his next shot. He wouldn't take anything for granted, even if he felt certain that Mackenzie was as crazy about him as he was about her.

"Keep your eye on the eight ball," he told Julius, then coolly slammed the cue ball into it and watched it bounce off the table and go into the pocket.

"I hear you're into gardening," Yasmine said, while showing off her greenhouse with a collection of exotic plants.

"Yes, I love playing with dirt and flowers," Mackenzie admitted, admiring the plants over a glass of wine.

"You might not guess from looking at this, but I don't have much of a green thumb. I had this done professionally."

"If you can afford it, why not?"

"True." Yasmine faced her. "Maybe you could make some suggestions on what flowers I could add to the garden?"

"I'd love to." Mackenzie was always happy to share some of her expertise with others.

After assessing the collection, she recommended tuberous begonias, scorpion orchids and chenille plants.

"I'll get them all," Yasmine promised.

Mackenzie recognized the lavender mountain lilies and pastel tulips and made a mental note to plant some in her own garden.

"So tell me about your son."

Mackenzie sipped her wine thoughtfully for a moment. "His name is Ryan. He's fifteen and living with his father in Los Angeles."

Yasmine smiled. "That must be really hard with him being so far away."

"Yes, it is sometimes," she conceded before adding, "but it was his choice."

"I can see that. What kid wouldn't want to live in sunny Southern California, if the opportunity presented itself?"

"Probably not many."

"Do you see him often?"

"I haven't seen him since he moved there more than six months ago." Mackenzie paused, wondering how much information she should divulge. After all, they were just getting to know each other. Sharing the fact that Ryan seemed to suddenly be bucking wanting to live in California might not be such a good idea considering that she hadn't as yet been as forthcoming with Ian on the matter, preferring to wait and see if this was only a passing phase for Ryan. "We do talk and see each other online," she noted, "and, of course, on the phone."

"That's good to hear." Yasmine brushed her hair to the side. "Julius and I are trying to have a child," she said quietly.

"Really?" Mackenzie's brow shot up with surprise.

"Yes. I'd like three or four. I think Julius would prefer one or two. We'll just work on the first one for now and see how things go from there."

"I'm happy for you." Mackenzie gave her a smile. "I hope you get pregnant soon."

"So do I. My sister just had her first child and loves him more than anything. I want that same feeling, as I'm sure you can understand."

Mackenzie sipped more wine. She did love Ryan, no matter

where he lived. She thought back to the joy of giving birth to him and the ensuing years of raising him, often by herself while his father was out of town. She had thought it might be nice to have another child someday, but only if the man she loved wanted one, too. That didn't seem to be the case with Ian.

Should I resent that?

She dismissed the notion, knowing full well that he had every right to feel the way he did about children. He was still a good man and one Mackenzie couldn't imagine not being in her life.

Even if it meant he might have to accept her son as his own someday.

Chapter 15

On Friday Mackenzie took the day off and went with Ian on a floating tour of the Lamoille River. It was her first time canoeing and she enjoyed being on the water on a sunny afternoon.

"You're doing great," Ian said, after showing her the proper way to paddle.

"Am I really?" She wondered if her arms would be able to hold up for the whole trip, as this workout was using different muscles than she was used to.

"Of course. You have a good teacher." He flashed a sexy smile and showed off his own muscular upper body at work. "Next time we can try our hand at kayaking."

"Okay by me." That was another adventure Mackenzie had yet to experience, but she would be happy to try. "What aren't you good at?"

"Singing." Ian laughed. "I can play the best music around

and listen to a lyrical voice like yours all day long, but I can't carry a tune even if my life depended on it."

"Fortunately it doesn't."

Mackenzie appreciated that Ian was at least willing to admit he was less than perfect, something most men seemed incapable of doing.

"I suppose you fish, too?"

He nodded. "I used to visit my uncle Bud in Mississippi every summer as a child. That was pretty much all he did when he wasn't working at the farm. He taught me well."

"So you spent part of your childhood on a farm?"

"Yeah. I really enjoyed feeding chickens, milking cows, riding ponies. The whole nine yards. Gives you a whole new appreciation for how the other half lives."

"I can only imagine." Mackenzie could probably count on one hand the number of times she had visited a farm. She'd never gotten the real flavor of farm life, but was completely open-minded and game to try anything once.

They eased up and floated slowly down the river, allowing themselves to experience the lush New England scenery, including spectacular views of the Green Mountains.

"I think I could stay out here all day," Ian said, his eyes focused on Mackenzie.

She felt the heat emanating from him. "So could I, as long as you were with me."

He grinned. "I think that can be arranged."

Ian leaned forward and kissed her, causing the canoe to tilt slightly. Mackenzie opened her mouth, loving his taste and the way he used his tongue.

Their lips remained locked seemingly forever but eventually their kiss ended. They enjoyed the rest of the afternoon on the water. Then they headed to the shore where they finished their outing with a wine- and cheese-tasting tour at a winery.

"To you and to a marvelous day together," Ian said, lifting his glass.

"Well said." Mackenzie clinked his glass and took a sip of the sweet white wine.

She couldn't remember a time when she felt so appreciated and connected.

Later that night Ian held Mackenzie up against the wall, kissing her feverishly while they made love. Her legs were wrapped securely around his waist and their hands clasped overhead. His erection throbbed as he went deeper and deeper inside Mackenzie, fighting the urge to release. He didn't want to let go till she was ready to climax.

The way her body shook wildly and soft murmurs came into his mouth told Ian the moment was near. He loved when they reached a climax simultaneously, for Mackenzie's powerful spasms left him incredibly aroused and wanting only to succumb to desire.

Mackenzie gripped Ian's head tightly and flattened his lips with luscious kisses. He pressed their chests together and cupped Mackenzie's firm buttocks, propelling himself in and out of her, caught in the throes of sexual bliss. He breathed in her intoxicating feminine scent, tasting the moist delights inside Mackenzie's mouth with a sense of urgency to take as much of her as he could.

Mackenzie cried out unevenly as her climax erupted. "Ian…please don't stop…"

"I won't," he promised with a gasp, plunging farther inside her with a passion.

"Oh…you feel so good…"

"You feel even better," he voiced huskily.

"Hmm…" She chewed on his lower lip. "Take me…I'm ready now—"

She opened up more, drawing him in, giving him free rein to catch up to her unbridled passion.

"Nothing on earth could stop me from taking all of you," he declared lasciviously.

He turned so his back was against the wall. Mackenzie straddled Ian, climbing farther up and sliding down his phallus ardently to urge him on. She kissed him left and right, up and down, putting her tongue in Ian's mouth while running her hands over his cheeks and shoulders sinuously.

Ian relinquished all self-control and felt his forceful release surge along with Mackenzie's. His eyes squeezed shut, body quavered, and his breathing accelerated while the moment took hold. Each clung to the other lustfully as their lovemaking brought them to new heights of ecstasy that neither wanted to escape.

On Saturday morning, Mackenzie lay naked in Ian's comforting and powerful arms, happily exhausted after spending the night together fulfilling each other's sexual desires from *A* to *Z*.

If they could stay this way forever it would be fine with her. She couldn't think of anywhere else she would rather be than with the man who had stolen her heart and so much more. Mackenzie wondered how she had been so fortunate to capture his attention in a way that told her he was every bit as sold on her as she was him. She didn't care to speculate too much, but rather she wanted to revel in what was happening, giving her a whole new and exciting reason to live.

When the phone chimed, Mackenzie snapped out of her reverie, but Ian remained sound asleep. She imagined he was dreaming about her—them—and what they had just spent hours doing and perfecting with each tantalizing touch of their bodies.

She extricated herself from Ian's embrace and slid out of

bed. Grabbing her cell phone, Mackenzie saw that it was Brent calling. Hopefully he'd gotten things resolved with Ryan so their son could get set to start school soon in L.A.

She glanced at Ian, still showing no sign of consciousness. After putting on her robe, Mackenzie stepped into the hall and went downstairs.

She sighed and answered the phone. "It took you long enough to get back to me."

"Sorry." He paused. "We've got a problem."

"What kind of problem?"

Another pause. "Ryan's run away."

"What?" Mackenzie's heart sank.

"We had a falling out and he just left," Brent voiced nervously.

"When was this?" she asked.

Brent hesitated. "Three days ago."

"Three days ago!" Mackenzie couldn't believe her ears. "And you're just telling me now?"

"I didn't want to worry you," he muttered.

"That wasn't your decision to make," she said unhappily.

"I was hoping I'd find him, or that he'd come back."

Mackenzie's temples throbbed with indignation. "You had no right to keep this from me! Ryan is my son, too."

Brent sighed. "I know, and I'm sorry."

She tried not to panic, suspecting that Ryan just needed to cool off. Wasn't this what many kids did these days to deal with stress?

Mackenzie's mouth became a straight line. "What did you say to him to make him leave?" she demanded of her ex.

"Only that it was time he grew up and stopped acting like the whole world revolved around him," Brent said sharply.

"Is that what *she* told you to say?"

"If you're referring to Deborah, no," Brent snapped. "I can speak my own mind, thank you."

"Well, you obviously went too far this time with your son."
Mackenzie wasn't convinced that his wife hadn't somehow
played a strong role in their son leaving home.

"I don't like this any more than you do. I only wanted to
talk some sense into him so he didn't keep trying to pit us
against each other."

"Is that what you think?"

"Don't you?" Brent voiced flatly. "How else do you ex-
plain his erratic behavior of late?"

"I really don't want to get into the blame game," Mackenzie stressed.

"That's not what I'm picking up. Seems like you've already
made up your mind that it's all my fault."

Mackenzie conceded this was exactly what she was thinking. She forced herself to take a step back and at least give
him the benefit of the doubt, hard as that was.

"Who's at fault is not really important right now," she indicated. "Our son is."

"You're right."

Mackenzie breathed out her nose. "Did you check with
his friends?"

"Yeah—at least the ones I'm aware of. So far no one seems
to know anything."

Mackenzie doubted that. Teenagers always talked to their
friends, especially if they were planning to run away from
home. Maybe Ryan was staying with one of them. At least,
she hoped that was the case.

"Did you call the police?" she asked.

"Yes, and they're supposed to be checking into it."

Supposed to be? That didn't sound very comforting.
"Either they are or they aren't."

"They've notified units to be on the lookout," he said shakily.

"Has an AMBER Alert been issued?"

"No," Brent muttered. "The police don't think this rises to that level, since Ryan left of his own accord and there's no sign of imminent danger."

"Why does the danger have to be imminent for our son to be helped by those who are being paid to serve the public?" Mackenzie lashed out. "He's out there who knows where and in trouble, whether he left home voluntarily, was thrown out or taken against his will."

"I agree with you," Brent replied understandingly. "But what more can I do…?"

Mackenzie was angry that the police weren't taking this seriously. For all she knew, Ryan could be badly injured somewhere and unable to communicate. Or, heaven forbid, maybe even dead. The thought left her numb.

She saw Ian come down the stairs, fully dressed. He flashed her a concerned look, as though he'd overheard some of the conversation.

Mackenzie had mixed emotions at that point, vacillating between being frightened to death for her son's welfare and concern for her relationship with her next-door neighbor, whose support she might need now more than ever. She found herself shaking.

Ian walked up and put his arms around her. She felt comforted by his embrace and distracted at the same time in knowing that Ryan's very life could be hanging in the balance. A sense of help-lessness tugged at Mackenzie. Along with the second-guessing for ever allowing him to leave Vermont in the first place.

"Are you still there?" Brent asked impatiently.

Mackenzie pushed the phone against her ear. "Yes, I'm here." *But where is our son?*

"I know this is asking a lot of you, but try not to worry."

"I can't do that," Mackenzie told him pointedly. "Not until I know Ryan is safe and sound."

"I'm sure he'll show up sooner or later," Brent said.

"And what if he doesn't?" she questioned.

"No reason to be pessimistic about this. Ryan did a stupid thing, but he's not stupid. He'll come back. In the mean time, we'll keep searching the places he hangs out and see what happens."

Ian gave her a squeeze and Mackenzie wondered what was going on in his head. She hoped none of this turned him off. Her focus right now, though, had to be her son and what could be a dire situation, bringing her to a decision.

"I'm coming out there," she announced to Brent, glancing up at Ian for a reaction. His brow rose crookedly.

"I don't think that's—" Brent began.

"It doesn't matter what you think." Mackenzie cut him off, expecting resistance to the idea of invading his perfect world. Only, it wasn't so perfect at the moment. "I have to do whatever I can to find our son. Obviously you haven't done enough."

Brent groaned. "What's that supposed to mean?"

She fought back tears. "You should have stopped him from leaving when you had the chance."

"How the hell was I supposed to know he'd do something foolish like this?"

"Maybe you should have anticipated it after siding with your wife over your own son!" Mackenzie accused him.

"Don't be ridiculous," Brent said defensively. "It has nothing to do with Deborah. This is about Ryan and his un-willingness to grow up."

Mackenzie scoffed at that. Ryan needed his father to act the part, and Brent didn't seem to get that.

Or am I being too unreasonable?

She found Ian's sympathetic gaze and realized it was time to bring him up-to-date on whatever he hadn't already figured out. She could only hope he would support her on this even after the shock wore off.

"I have to go," she told Brent, suspecting he'd heard enough of her ranting and raving for the time being. "If you hear anything, please let me know."

"I will," he promised tersely.

Mackenzie disconnected, wondering where her son was and praying he was okay.

Chapter 16

Ian had quickly gotten the gist of the story. Apparently Mackenzie's son had run away from home and the police were doing little, if anything, to find him. Ian wondered what would cause Ryan to take such drastic measures. Didn't he realize there were consequences for putting his parents through hell and possibly endangering himself? Mackenzie had lashed out at her ex and his new wife, while putting little blame on the runaway for his actions.

Ian recognized how rebellious kids could be at that age, having more than once seriously considered bolting himself when his parents seemed unreasonable. Looking back, he realized it had been the other way around. He had thought he was grown and pretty much rejected much of what his parents were trying to teach him about responsibility and becoming a man.

Was that the case with Mackenzie's son, too? Or were other forces at work that had yet to be revealed?

"Sounds pretty serious," Ian said, narrowing his eyes while wanting Mackenzie to fill in the blanks.

"It could be." Mackenzie's voice shook. "Ryan's run away, and right now his father doesn't have a clue where he might be."

Ian tried to ignore her in a pink kimono robe with obviously nothing on underneath. Now was not the time to think sexually. Not with Mackenzie clearly scared to death about her son and his whereabouts.

Ian held her. "It's going to be all right," he said softly, knowing this wasn't necessarily going to be the case. He felt helpless, having no experience with kids. He wasn't quite sure what soothing words to say to Mackenzie. *Maybe I should just stay out of it,* he thought, fearful of doing more harm than good by giving her false reassurances.

But how the hell could he, when the woman who stole his heart was in obvious panic mode?

"I can only hope so," Mackenzie cried on his shoulder. "If anything bad should happen to Ryan—"

"Let's not go there," Ian said, trying to keep himself together under the first real sign of strain since they had become a couple. "Have you tried his cell phone?"

Mackenzie batted her lashes musingly. "No. I was so caught up in this that I…"

"Maybe you should give it a try." Ian spoke gently.

"What if he's decided to shut himself off from everyone?" she asked.

"If Ryan sees it's you, he might pick up. Or, at worst, you can leave him a message to call as soon as he gets it."

"You're right."

Mackenzie called his number and let it ring till the voice mail picked up.

"Ryan, it's Mom. Please call when you get this and let me know you're all right. Your dad and Deborah are worried, too." She paused. "I love you."

"If he still has his cell phone, he'll get the message," Ian said optimistically. He preferred not to consider that this still might not be enough for a headstrong, rebellious kid to do the right thing and call her back.

"And what if he doesn't?" Mackenzie's eyes met Ian's with dread. "How do I deal with this if Ryan ends up on the streets of L.A., picked up by a pimp, forced to sell his body, becomes hooked on drugs, or even worse?"

"There's no reason to assume the worst-case scenario."

Mackenzie sucked in a deep breath. "I tend to do that when a stressful situation arises. I don't know why."

"Has Ryan ever done anything like this before?" asked Ian, curious.

Mackenzie leveled bold eyes at him. "Never!"

"He's never gone off in a huff after having a disagreement with you or your ex?"

She gave him a sober look. "Of course he has, just like most kids when they don't get their way."

"This could well be the same thing, more or less," Ian suggested.

"It's completely different," Mackenzie countered. "This has clearly been building for a while now."

"Has it?"

"Yes. He called me and asked to come home. I put him off when he was crying for help." Her eyes watered. "Now he's taken matters into his own hands."

"This is not your fault," Ian insisted, fearing this was spiraling out of control before the facts were even laid out. "You had no way of knowing Ryan would run away from home."

"The signs were there," she contended.

"What signs?"

Mackenzie sighed. "He's been in fights."

"Kids fight all the time," Ian said, having been there. "It's rarely serious. Certainly not to the level of running away from home."

"Ryan said that his dad and stepmom argued all the time over him. He was feeling the pressure of being an outsider, trying to measure up to something he wasn't."

Ian took a breath. "He was not an outsider to his father. Kids have to make adjustments all the time in living with one parent or the other. It doesn't mean they need to be coddled by the noncustodial parent in order to stay put. Especially if the child chose to go live with his father."

Mackenzie's eyes narrowed. "I'm not sure I like where this is heading."

"It's not heading anywhere," Ian said, seeking to defuse the situation. The last thing he needed was to try to come between Mackenzie and her missing child. On the other hand, someone needed to be the voice of reason here. "All I'm saying is you're not to blame for this. It could have happened whether he was in L.A. or Cheri Village."

"None of this changes the fact that my son is missing and he has to be found," Mackenzie said.

"He's only missing to you and his father—which isn't the same thing as missing altogether." Ian put an arm around her shoulder. "My guess is that he's somewhere safe, but just doesn't want to communicate with anyone right now."

"If not, then when?" Mackenzie's brow furrowed. "He must know we're worried to death about him."

"Kids don't always think about the implications of what they're doing," Ian told her. "I certainly didn't way back when. Only what works at the moment."

She pulled away from him. "Thanks for your input, but I

need to go to L.A.," she said. "Just sitting around waiting and not knowing anything will drive me crazy."

"You should if that will make you feel better." Ian seriously questioned the wisdom of flying across the country prematurely for something that could be little more than a misunderstanding between father and son. But that wasn't his call. He wanted to do anything to support Mackenzie. Even if that meant having to do without her company for a time while she got this issue resolved. Then a better thought entered Ian's head. "I'll go with you."

Her lashes fluttered. "I couldn't let you do that."

"You're not letting me," he stressed. "I want to do it."

"But what about your job?" Mackenzie paused. "Or Otis?"

"I haven't taken a day off since I started. This is a good time to use a couple of free days." Ian took her hand. "I'm sure I can get someone to dogsit. I'd just like to be there to support you through this, no matter how it turns out."

Mackenzie smiled through her tears. "Thank you for being so special and understanding." She put her arms around his waist. "I mean it."

Ian kissed the top of her head. "No thanks are necessary. I know you'd do the same were the situation reversed." He tried to imagine being a dad and having to deal with crises that had always been on someone else. Maybe this was what it meant to be a parent. He couldn't hold that against her even if Ian hadn't given much thought to something that had little bearing on his current relationship with Mackenzie. If this was to work he would have to accept that. Even if it meant having to always play second fiddle whenever her son got in trouble.

"Yes, I would," she said succinctly. "You've come to mean that much to me."

"Likewise."

Mackenzie turned her face up and kissed him. He returned

the kiss, remembering how they had spent much of the night before reality sank in.

Ian heard what sounded like a key in the front door. He released Mackenzie, and they both looked in that direction.

In a moment the door opened.

Ian's eyes popped wide as he recognized the tall, lanky boy he'd seen in the photograph. It was Mackenzie's son, Ryan.

Chapter 17

Mackenzie could only stare as she watched Ryan walk in the door as casually as if he'd just returned from another day at school. He looked tired and bedraggled in an oversize L.A. Lakers jersey and fleece shorts.

She pulled the robe tighter against her body. "What are you doing here?" she asked, feeling both relief and ill at ease.

He shrugged. "I told you I wanted to come home."

Mackenzie glanced at Ian, who was expressionless, and back to Ryan. "Why didn't you answer your cell phone?"

"I didn't want to talk to anyone," he responded tartly.

She drew her brows together. "You should have called! Your father and I have been worried sick about you."

"Yeah, right." Ryan rolled his eyes. "Is that why nobody wanted to listen to what I had to say?"

"I've always listened to you." Or she'd tried to.

"No, you haven't."

"Since when?" she challenged him, fighting to keep from crying again in knowing he was safe.

"You didn't listen when I told you I didn't want to live in L.A. anymore."

"That's because you never bothered to tell me why," Mackenzie said. "I did everything I could to get you to open up."

"I didn't feel like talking about it." He rubbed his nose. "Still don't."

"It's not that simple, young man," she said snappily, not wanting to let him off the hook after what he'd put them through. She didn't necessarily want to hash this out in front of Ian. But Mackenzie supposed he should know exactly what he was getting himself into if they were to embark on a long-term relationship. "I let you move to California earlier this year because this was what you wanted. Now you don't?"

Ryan's nose wrinkled. "Things change."

"You're right, they do," Mackenzie allowed. "And with those changes comes responsibility. It's time you learned what that's all about."

"Whatever," he said with a sneer.

Mackenzie bit her tongue. She wondered what to do with him. She certainly couldn't throw him out on the street. Or have him locked up for traveling across the country by himself, she assumed, without bothering to notify either parent. But he had to be held accountable for poor decision-making and showing a lack of respect for his parents. Nothing from this point on would be easy.

She noted he was staring at Ian and vice versa, reminding her that the two had not been introduced. It was hardly the way she had wanted them to meet. Sometimes life threw you a curve. The best she could hope for at this point was that they were at least civilized to each other. And that Ian didn't head for the hills, in spite of his kindness in offering to accompany her to L.A.

"This is Ian. He's my new next-door neighbor." Mackenzie shifted her gaze. "My son, Ryan."

"Hey, Ryan," Ian said in a deep voice, extending a hand.

Ryan hesitantly raised his long, thin arm. "Hi."

Mackenzie sighed. *At least that was a first step. Now, where do I go from here?*

Ian peered at Ryan. "You scared the hell out of your mother with this stunt you pulled."

"Excuse me…" Ryan's mouth hung open.

"You heard me. By doing such a boneheaded thing as walking out on your dad and stepmother, then giving your mother a conniption with this running-away-from-home bit, all you've shown is that you've got a lot more growing up to do."

Ryan's nostrils flared. "What would you know about it?"

"More than you think," Ian said harshly. "I know that had I done what you did at fifteen, my old man would've made sure I didn't simply get to walk away with a smug look on my face."

Ryan gave a sardonic chuckle. "That's not my problem."

"I know. Your problem is that you're too dumb to know you have a problem. When you do things like what you did, it affects more than you and your whims. All you had to do was phone Mackenzie and let her know what you were up to. But no, that went against the grain. So you did it your way—to hell with everyone else."

"I don't have to listen to this!" Ryan glared at Mackenzie. "Tell him to leave. Or do you want me to go…?"

Mackenzie gulped. She was stunned that Ian had taken Ryan to task like that. She hadn't seen it coming and had mixed emotions. There was no question that her son needed a verbal lashing, if only to get him to think about such actions in the future. But in the process, Ian had only complicated things as it related to establishing a relationship with Ryan. Or was this an indication that such a bond might be impossible for a man who had shown little interest in having children of his own?

She met Ian's hard gaze. "I think maybe you'd better go."

"I think you're right." He sighed and favored Ryan with a look. "For your mother's sake, I'm happy you made it here in one piece. You'd be surprised at just how many runaway teens end up anywhere other than where they wanted to be." Ian eyed Mackenzie again. "I'll see you later."

"All right." She flashed Ian a tiny smile, appreciating his candidness and take-charge approach more than she could say. Though she hated to see Ian leave, Mackenzie felt it was best that she talk to Ryan alone. "I'll call you."

Ian nodded. She watched him walk past Ryan, who looked ready to blow a fuse, and hadn't moved from his spot since coming in, as though still trying to decide if he would be welcome or not.

Mackenzie steadied herself for the uncertain road to follow. There was little question that some hard decisions would have to be made, affecting all parties involved. Ryan had somehow found his way home and now she had to deal with it. She could only hope that she had the inner strength to do what was right, whatever that happened to be.

Mackenzie believed that if she and Ian could get through this and still be a couple, they could probably get through anything. She remained cautiously optimistic that they were solid enough to withstand the ups and downs of motherhood and adolescence. But for now, her preoccupation had to be with Ryan and where they went from there.

Ian fed Otis, still shaken by the surprise of seeing Mackenzie's runaway son show up at her front door, acting as though the weight of the world were on his shoulders. It was a scene Ian hadn't been prepared for, and he wasn't sure he'd handled it properly when put to the test. *Was I too hard on the boy? Or not hard enough?* Did Mackenzie view that as unwanted meddling? Or a needed helping hand for a son whose respect for her was sorely lacking.

Ian contemplated the situation further after leaving Otis to eat by himself. The truth was that most kids today exaggerated their problems. Never mind the fact that they'd had life handed to them on a silver platter. Though Ian did not know the particulars of Ryan's decision to bolt from Southern California, he suspected it had less to do with maltreatment and more to do with never really giving his new environment a chance to work, as if that took more effort than he was willing to put out.

Evidently now Ryan had decided he wanted to live in Cheri Village again with Mackenzie, regardless of her feelings or life she'd started in his absence.

Will Mackenzie send him back to California to live with his father? Ian asked himself with more than a little curiosity. Or would she reclaim her son and the responsibility of raising a teenage boy who seemed in need of perhaps more supervision than she could muster?

Ian wondered where it would leave him, not to mention their relationship. Admittedly, he had become spoiled by Mackenzie's undivided attention, and was enjoying the fact that they'd been able to come and go as they pleased from house to house, day and night. The rules would obviously have to change with a teenager in the household. Ian wasn't sure just how much of a change he could handle. Or if he should have to adapt more to Ryan than the other way around.

I have to keep an open mind and not allow Ryan's presence, temporary or not, to distract from what Mackenzie and I are all about.

Ian was determined to keep a proper perspective. The

way he'd felt before about women with children had changed once he got to know Mackenzie, albeit as a woman with no "live-in" kids.

He would meet Ryan more than halfway and seriously try to get to know him, assuming the boy wasn't on the next plane back to L.A. already. Ian sensed that he was there to stay, for better or worse.

"Are you hungry?" Mackenzie asked after throwing on a boat-neck pullover and Bermuda shorts.

Ryan had finally unloaded the backpack from his broad shoulders.

"Yeah." He scratched his head of closely cropped black hair.

"Why don't you go wash up and I'll fix you something."

He nodded. "All right."

Mackenzie went into the kitchen to see what leftovers she could put together. She couldn't believe the emotional rollercoaster ride Ryan had taken her and Brent on. Had Ryan even considered for one moment the stress and strain he had caused them?

What is Ian thinking now, she wondered. *What isn't he thinking?*

He had handled the shock of Ryan's sudden appearance quite well. Was it just a facade, with Ian ready to back away from her family drama as soon as he walked out the door?

By the time Ryan came into the kitchen, Mackenzie had warmed some leftover chicken, rice and greens.

She sipped coffee, while watching him devour the food as though he hadn't eaten in a month.

"How did you get here?" She was almost afraid to ask, but she needed some explanation if she was going to be able to help her son.

"Took a bus," Ryan muttered tonelessly.

"And you couldn't call to tell me you were coming?" Her chest rose. "I could have at least picked you up at the station."

He looked away. "I was afraid you'd tell me not to get on the bus—that there's no place for me here anymore."

Mackenzie's heart nearly tore in half. "There's always a place for you in this house," she said.

"Didn't sound like it last time we talked."

"I never said you couldn't come back home. I just felt it wasn't the right thing to do under the circumstances."

"It felt right to me," he muttered.

"That may be. But just leaving your dad and stepmother without telling them or anyone else where you were going was dumb and dangerous." Mackenzie paused so as not to sound overly harsh. "We taught you better than that."

"I'm sorry, but I didn't know what else to do."

"You could have stayed there and talked your problems through with your father."

Ryan voraciously bit into a chicken thigh. "He doesn't care about me—only her."

"That's not true." In spite of the strained relations between her and Brent, Mackenzie did not believe for one second that Brent didn't want what was best for his son. Certainly he would never have condoned Ryan's decision to hop on a bus and ride across the country without a word to anyone.

"You weren't there," Ryan said brusquely.

"No, I wasn't. But you were by your own choice. Running away only complicates things—it doesn't solve them."

He tilted his face. "Are you saying I can't stay?"

Mackenzie considered the question.

What am I saying? Should I just give in again after all we went through to get him settled in California? If Ryan changes his mind in another six months, where will that leave me?

She sucked in a deep breath. "I'm saying that we need to talk about this. You, me, your dad and stepmom."

He frowned. "Why can't it just be you and me?"

"Because it doesn't work that way. This affects all of us. You're welcome to stay here for now until we all get together and decide what's best."

"Who for?" He sneered. "Dad and Deborah? Or you and the tough-guy neighbor?"

Mackenzie regarded him sharply. "This isn't about me and Ian." Or maybe it was to some degree, but certainly not the central issue. "Your best interests are what's most important, even if you may not agree."

He raised a brow. "So what are you doing with him?"

She hadn't intended to get into her relationship with Ian just yet, preferring to focus more on Ryan's unexpected presence. But since the two issues were connected to one degree or another, she saw no reason to postpone it.

"We have started dating."

Ryan nodded. "Yeah, I figured as much, the way he was looking at you and barking at me."

Mackenzie suddenly felt self-conscious. She had dated before when Ryan was still living there after the divorce. But it had never been with someone she'd fallen head over heels for and wanted her son to like.

And vice versa.

"Ian is a good man who cares a lot about me," she emphasized. "That includes offering his two cents in trying to stand up for what he believes is right."

"You can do better than him," Ryan said sneeringly.

Mackenzie's lips pursed. "Thanks, but I don't need your permission to decide who to date any more than your dad did when he made his choice to marry Deborah."

"Well, Dad made a mistake," he grumbled. "He should've stayed with you instead of marrying that witch."

"We've already been through this. Your father and I had some differences, but we've both moved on and you have to accept that."

Mackenzie fought off the memories that still smarted. For the longest time she had blamed herself to some extent for a cheating spouse, as many wives probably did. Maybe if she'd given Brent more of what he wanted or less of what he didn't want, he would have stayed true to their marriage. And maybe Ryan wouldn't be moving back and forth between them on a whim while searching for guidance. But the truth was Mackenzie wasn't at fault for Brent's weaknesses and penchant for wanting to walk both sides of the street. She had too much self-respect to allow him to get away with it. So she'd given him up to another woman and saw it as the best thing that ever happened to her.

Ryan finished the last of his meal, his silence a mute protest.

"Go get some sleep now. We'll talk about this later."

"Yeah, I can hardly wait."

Mackenzie sucked in a deep breath but did not respond. She was not going to get into it with him, aware that he was being a typical teen. She was just happy that he was safe.

The next step was to decide whether or not he'd be moving back in.

As soon as Ryan had closed the door to his room, Mackenzie called Brent to let him know what was happening.

"Ryan's here."

"What?"

"He took the bus."

Brent muttered an expletive. "Do you want me to come and get him?"

"What I'd like is for you, me and Deborah to get together to talk about why he left and what we can do to make sure it doesn't happen again, no matter where he's living."

"Yeah, that's a good idea. Just give us a few days to make travel arrangements."

Mackenzie agreed, as if there were a choice. She was glad that Brent saw eye to eye with her on this one, rather than rant and rave as had been the case so often during their marriage. Maybe Deborah had softened him somewhat. Regardless, Mackenzie was still worried that Deborah's feelings toward Ryan were a different matter and may be at the core of why he'd run away. On the other hand, it was also plausible that her son had acted impulsively for reasons none of them were privy to.

"So it's okay if he stays with you in the meantime?" Brent asked.

"Of course. Although he's been living with you, this is also Ryan's home."

"Good." He paused. "Do you need any money?"

"I only need you to get here so we can resolve this as quickly and painlessly as possible."

"Absolutely. I understand."

After hanging up, Mackenzie gave in to her strong desire to hear Ian's voice. She wanted to get some perspective on where his head was after Ryan's impromptu return. She pushed Ian's speed-dial number and recalled the few times they'd turned each other on with some romance talk over the phone. That was something she never would have contemplated before. But with Ian anything seemed possible, fun, romantic and sexy. She didn't want to lose that bond, especially when the potential for so much more was there.

"Hey there," Ian answered, sounding cheerful.

"Hope I'm not calling at a bad time?"

"You're not."

"So I'm sure you weren't expecting Ryan to just show up like that."

"Were you?"

Mackenzie sighed. "No."

"Didn't think so."

"But now that he's here, I have to figure out what's going to happen with him."

"I understand," Ian said.

"Do you?" *How can you possibly understand the trials and tribulations of parenthood if you aren't a parent?*

"Yeah, pretty much. Your son shows up out of the blue and is ready to move back in with you."

"How do you feel about that?" Mackenzie thought she might as well get right to the heart of the matter.

Ian waited a moment before responding. "I'm not sure how I feel, to tell you the truth. I guess it was easier to think of you as a mother when your son was on the other side of the country."

"I've always been a mother," she stressed. "I never made a secret of that, even with Ryan living in California."

"I know. I didn't mean it like that," Ian said and then sighed. "So will he be living with you full-time now?"

"I don't know." She paused. "Ryan's father will be coming in a few days so we can sort this whole thing out."

"I thought it had already been sorted out."

"So did I. But things have changed...."

"Are you really going to let a fifteen-year-old boy dictate the way things ought to be?" Ian's voice had a hard edge to it.

"It will be decided by committee," Mackenzie said.

"Does that include me? Or am I not part of the equation on deciding his future...or our future?"

Mackenzie swallowed, feeling pressure from all sides. The worst-case scenario was losing the man she'd fallen in love with because he couldn't handle having her son around. At the same time, Mackenzie could not abandon Ryan and his needs, no matter what. As a mother, she had to act in his best interest, even if that meant sacrificing her relationship with Ian.

"I want us to have a future with all my heart, Ian. But the decision about Ryan has to be made by the people who are responsible for his health and well-being. Right now that doesn't include you. I hope you can respect that and don't take it personally, or allow it to have a negative impact on our relationship."

Ian remained silent for a long moment.

"I'm sorry if I want you all to myself," he muttered unapologetically.

"I feel the same way about you." Mackenzie had gotten used to the time they'd been able to spend alone together. But she was a mother first and that would never change.

"We have to be realistic, though. Ryan's having some issues right now and I need to be there for him. Once this is resolved, maybe things can go back to how they were with us."

"Are you saying you want to stop seeing each other?"

That wasn't what she meant. But maybe it would be the best thing for everyone, at least temporarily. It wouldn't be fair to Ian or Ryan if Mackenzie's loyalties were divided and both relationships suffered in the process.

Or would suspending my involvement with Ian prove to be the biggest mistake of my life?

"I'm only saying that I ask you to be patient," she told him. "I know it's asking a lot. I just need to get through this with Ryan. Whatever happens, I want things to work out for you and me."

"I want that, too." He sighed into the phone. "Take as much time as you need," Ian said sincerely.

"Do you mean it?"

"Yeah. It's probably a good idea if we both take a step back to see how this plays out."

Mackenzie wasn't sure she liked the tone of that. Was this some type of reverse psychology where he was dumping her without seeming like the bad guy? Or was she looking for something that wasn't there?

"Do what you need to do," she said.

"You, too."

When Mackenzie hung up, she felt as if their relationship had suddenly hit a brick wall, with no guarantee the magic that had brought them together with such passion would ever return.

Chapter 18

On Monday morning, Ian did his radio show, trying to maintain his usual upbeat attitude about life. But he suspected the listeners could sense all was not fine and dandy in his world. Far from it. But he blamed much of it on himself.

How could he have been so selfish with Mackenzie? Had he really expected to have a place at the table in deciding her son's fate? And was he out of line in wanting Mackenzie to put his needs ahead of her son's?

Ian wondered if he might not be using her predicament merely as an excuse to back out of a situation he was not comfortable with. Having a teenager in the picture scared him. He didn't feel he was qualified to give advice in a fatherly way. Nor was he eager to try to keep the boy in line, especially when his own father couldn't do it. But Ian pushed these thoughts aside. He didn't want this to get the better of him. It was too soon to assume the worst or make decisions he might regret later.

The one thing Ian couldn't deny was that he had developed strong feelings for Mackenzie that weren't likely to go away. He was pretty sure the same was true for her. Would this be enough to keep their relationship from falling to pieces before his very eyes?

Mackenzie had made a point to listen to Ian on the radio that morning. She wondered if there might be a hint in his words as to how he was feeling. Perhaps the nuances might reveal something their conversation hadn't.

Instead, she detected he was ill at ease. He seemed to be full of ambiguities, which Mackenzie was experiencing herself. She doubted this would change until after she knew where things stood with Ryan and apparently Ian was caught in the same vortex. She wouldn't ask him to stay in their relationship if he felt uncomfortable having her son around. But nothing would make Mackenzie happier than if Ian were there for her, and supported her through whatever decision she came to about Ryan. She could only maintain a positive attitude and believe that her knight in shining armor would not wind up being a frog when all was said and done.

Mackenzie decided to go into work late, wanting to make adjustments in the house for Ryan's presence, even if it wound up being short-lived. She made him a breakfast of waffles and bacon, almost forgetting that a still-growing teenage boy could eat three or four times as much as anyone else.

"I won't have to go back, will I?" Ryan asked, overloading his waffles with syrup.

"I don't know." Mackenzie wouldn't commit to anything prematurely, especially when she still didn't know the root of his problems. "Whether you like it or not, you've made a life in L.A. Moving back here means changing schools again, zip codes and everything in between."

"It won't be that hard."

"Maybe not for you, but your dad and I went through a lot to get you relocated to California. It will take more than a change of heart after only a few months to get us to reverse course. Can you understand that?"

"Yeah, I guess so." He shrugged, lifting a glass of orange juice. "I never really wanted to move there."

Mackenzie cocked a brow. "What? I seem to recall you couldn't get away from here—from me and my mothering you—fast enough. Or have you conveniently forgotten that?"

Ryan leaned back in his chair. "It wasn't about you," he said thoughtfully. "I just needed to get away."

"Why?"

He paused. "My girlfriend."

Mackenzie's mind tried to pinpoint which girl he was talking about, as there had seemed to be so many.

She finally gave up. "Help me out here."

"Gail Pineford."

Mackenzie rolled her eyes. "Since when?" She recalled that Gail had a bad reputation and seemed out of Ryan's league.

"Since like forever."

"You never mentioned—"

"I don't tell you everything about who I hang out with."

"Apparently not." She sipped her coffee, wondering who he'd hung out with in L.A. "So what exactly happened with Gail to make you want to leave?"

"She dumped me." He frowned and said, "And I guess I just couldn't deal with seeing her every single day at school with Adam Franklin hanging all over her."

"What makes you think you'll be able to handle it now?" Mackenzie asked, unconvinced.

Ryan grabbed a piece of bacon. "I'm over her now and I just want my life back."

"What about the friends you made in L.A.?"

"We can keep in touch over the phone and online."

Mackenzie was concerned that Ryan left home to run away from Gail. And now he was running away from California in what was becoming a disturbing pattern.

"Did you ever think about the fact that I might have made a life for myself since you've been gone?"

Ryan looked up at her. "You mean with Ian?"

"I mean in every way," she answered, not wanting to make it all about Ian, even if he'd been the biggest change in her life. "I've gotten used to being on my own because you decided California was where you'd rather be. Now you've come back home without bothering to tell anyone. How do I know you won't run to L.A. again if I—we—let you stay here?"

Ryan sucked in a deep breath. "Because this is where I belong," he said simply.

Mackenzie contemplated the notion while wondering if he and Ian could coexist in her world. Would Ryan find reasons not to like Ian in the same way that he and Deborah didn't get along? And what about Ian's admission that he wasn't "daddy material"? Mackenzie had taken that to mean he didn't want to be involved with someone who had a child living at home. Would she need to sacrifice her relationship with the most wonderful man she'd ever met if he couldn't accept that her son would need to be part of Ian's life, too, in order to make this work?

In the afternoon, Ian and Doug met for beers at a place near the radio station. Ian needed someone to vent to in what had been an unexpected turn of events in his relationship with Mackenzie. Doug volunteered for the job, even offering to buy the drinks.

"So you're telling me her son just walked in without warning, ready to move home for good?" Doug looked across the table at Ian.

"Yeah, that's about the size of it," he said before sipping the foam off his beer.

"After running away from California?"

"You got it."

Doug tugged at his newly grown, neatly trimmed beard. "Wow."

"Yeah, wow," muttered Ian, refraining from using harsher language.

"Well, has your lady given you a clue as to what she plans to do about this little predicament?"

"She and her ex are going to evaluate it and weigh their options."

"Meaning he could be home to stay?" Doug surmised.

"That's a possibility," Ian allowed, instincts telling him that their carefree existence as a couple was over.

"How do you feel about that?"

He sighed. "I guess I'll just have to accept it."

"Doesn't sound very encouraging."

Ian looked away and back. "I want Mackenzie to be happy. If it means taking her son in, so be it."

"But what will make you happy?"

Ian swallowed some beer and wiped his mouth. "Being with the woman I love."

He wasn't afraid to voice his emotions. The reality was no one had ever captured his heart the way Mackenzie had. She meant the world to Ian and, no matter what, he didn't want to lose her.

"Then go be with her."

Ian grabbed a handful of peanuts. "I can't. We both agreed to take some time off until she comes to a conclusion about her son."

"I see." Doug lifted his mug. "Do you think she loves you, too?"

Ian wanted to believe she did, though neither of them had come right out and said so. "Yes, I'm pretty sure the feelings are mutual."

"In that case, you should be able to work your way through whatever happens with the kid and move forward."

Ian wanted to agree. But that didn't stop him from wondering if he and Mackenzie were still on the same page with regard to their relationship. What if having her son around meant Mackenzie would lose part of herself in the process— the part that was playful, sexual, full of life and excitingly unpredictable? Could something like that really happen? Ian was afraid to find out.

Chapter 19

Mackenzie vowed that she wouldn't go after Deborah for contributing to the breakup of her marriage, or even for her role in making Ryan's life in California less than satisfying. This would only create more conflict and drama that neither she nor Ryan needed. Her only desire was to deal with the issues at hand and get them resolved as soon as possible, for the sake of everyone involved. Until that happened, Mackenzie wanted to be civilized in communicating with her guests.

Everyone was seated in the living room. Mackenzie occupied the French Louis XV love seat. Ryan looked uncomfortable on the solid-wood accent chair. Brent and Deborah sat on the antique fringed sofa. They were holding hands as if to remind Mackenzie of what she wanted to forget.

Deborah, all of twenty-five, looked older, with too much makeup and layered, curly sable hair that was ill-suited for the shape of her face. At forty-one, Brent was around Ian's height, but not as fit. His hair was graying and short. He shot Ryan an angry look, as if he'd kept his temper in check long enough.

"What the hell were you thinking just taking off like that? You made everyone crazy not knowing if you were dead or alive or what happened."

Ryan shrunk back into the chair. "I didn't want to be there anymore."

"It's not your decision, boy. As your parents, we're responsible for where you live and everything else that goes on in your life."

"She wouldn't get off my back," Ryan spat out, aiming narrowed eyes at Deborah.

She batted her false lashes. "All I tried to do was instill some rules for you to follow while you were living under our roof. But you made it twice as hard on yourself as you needed to."

Brent put his arm around her supportively. "You think you're grown up, but what you did was totally immature and unacceptable."

"It's a bit late for the blame game," Mackenzie said, feeling she needed to be the voice of reason. "What's done is done. We need to decide where to go from here."

"I think we should take him back to L.A.," Brent said, ignoring the disapproving gaze of his wife.

Ryan's nostrils flared in protest. "I don't want to live with you anymore."

"Maybe we shouldn't force him to go back," argued Deborah.

Brent grunted. "He needs to learn that he's not calling the shots here."

"Mom…" Ryan flashed Mackenzie a pleading look to intervene.

She felt put on the spot, wanting to do the right thing while weighing the consequences of her decision. Mackenzie thought about Ian. She wished he were there, if only for support and to even up the playing field. She wondered if she could count on him to be there for her when the chips were down.

"He can stay here…." Mackenzie heard herself say.

Brent's eyes narrowed. "Are you sure you know what you're getting yourself into?"

"Probably not," she conceded.

The fact that Ryan was nearing sixteen and maturing physically and mentally made Mackenzie concerned that it might be too much for her to handle alone. But it wouldn't be long until he was off to college and at least if he was back, living with her, Mackenzie could better help him achieve his full potential in school. And she doubted Brent would complain much, knowing he would be pleasing his young wife with Ryan out of her too-dry hair.

"He can spend the summers in L.A., if he wants," Mackenzie offered hopefully. "Maybe things will still work out so Ryan can go to UCLA after he graduates."

Brent's tight face softened. "If that's what you want."

"Not necessarily," she said honestly. "It is what it is. I just think it's the best solution at this time."

Brent looked over to his son. "What do you think, Ryan?"

"I agree."

"Not so fast," Mackenzie said, not wanting him to think he had the upper hand. "There are a few stipulations. First, there will be no more moving back and forth between us on a whim, or when there are misunderstandings or you don't get your way. Understood?"

He cracked a smile. "Yeah."

"Also, I expect you to do your homework, pick up after yourself and not count on me to be your maid, and treat whomever I choose to date with more respect than I think you've shown Deborah." Mackenzie met her eyes in a show of unity, getting a warm smile in return, before resting her gaze on Ryan. "Are we clear?"

He nodded and lost the smile. "Yeah, we're clear."

She considered that a victory of sorts in taking a preemptive strike against him slipping back into his old, unacceptable ways. Or making it difficult for Ian or any other man to get close to her. Now she could only hope Ian would be willing to give a little, too by accepting her son and giving their relationship a chance to grow even more.

"In that case it's settled," she told Ryan. "You can stay."

"Thanks," he said sheepishly.

Mackenzie suppressed a smile. "Just remember, I'm holding you to everything we agreed on."

She saw this as a good first step toward resolving the issue. She'd work on Ian next, assuming their relationship hadn't already ended.

"Are you seeing someone?" Brent regarded Mackenzie curiously in the kitchen while Deborah had gone to the bathroom.

Mackenzie debated whether or not to satisfy his snooping. Could he be jealous? Wasn't his second wife enough to hold his attention?

"As a matter of fact, I am," she told him, even if they had agreed on a break until Ryan's living situation had been decided.

"Anyone I know?"

She watched the grin play on his lips. "No."

"Oh." Brent took a sip from his bottled water. "Well, I'm happy for you, and I hope it works out."

"You do?" Her lashes flickered.

"Of course. You're still a beautiful woman that any man would love to be with."

Mackenzie thought of Ian and how well they seemed to fit

together. She wondered if their relationship might someday blossom into marriage. Or was that wishful thinking?

"We'll see what happens." She smoothed an eyebrow. "Deborah seems to really suit you."

Brent nodded appreciatively. "Thanks. She's got a good heart."

"I hope you can make this marriage work."

"I intend to."

Mackenzie was willing to give him the benefit of the doubt, while hoping that Deborah and Ryan could learn to see eye to eye. She wanted her son to feel as welcome visiting his dad as when he was home in Cheri Village. Family unity was important to Mackenzie, no matter where the family lived. She realized now that this connection was something that had been missing in her life since the divorce. Though she had enjoyed the freedom of being single, Mackenzie wanted even more the intimate bond of matrimony and maybe even another child. But only if her partner agreed to it wholeheartedly.

Chapter 20

Ian listened as Emily gave the traffic report. As usual, nothing out of the ordinary. Plenty of rush-hour traffic, but no accidents or breakdowns to mar the morning commute.

While waiting his turn, Ian thought about Mackenzie. He hadn't spoken to her in more than a week and missed her terribly. He had caught a glimpse of a forty-something man and a younger woman arriving at her house and assumed it was Mackenzie's ex and his wife there to hammer out the details of Ryan's immediate future.

Ian had considered calling Mackenzie more than once to offer support for whatever she decided. Instead he chose to stay on the sidelines and not put undue pressure on her. She had to do what was best for her family. And since he wasn't a part of it, Ian kept his distance.

Maybe I've gone about it the wrong way.

The reality was Mackenzie had been the closest thing to a

family that Ian had ever known in his adult life. Things had reached the point between them where they could finish each other's sentences. That told him she was someone far too special to let get away. He had yet to get to know Ryan. He seemed like a decent enough kid, albeit with typical adolescent rebellion.

If I get the chance, I'd like to spend some time with him. Maybe he could teach me a thing or two about what it takes to bond with a teenager these days.

Or would Mackenzie want to move in a new direction now if her son was home permanently? Ian longed for her touch and the invigorating smell of Mackenzie's soft skin. He missed making love to her until the wee hours of the morning. Even just talking to her was something he had started to take for granted. Now he would give anything to get that back.

When the commercial break ended, Ian took the microphone.

"Can a day begin any more glorious than this with the sun already shining brightly? I'm not one for cloudy skies. It's too depressing. Here's a song that should brighten anyone's mood, by Michelle Conte, a wonderfully talented jazz artist reminiscent of a lady I know. It's called 'I Thought About You.'"

"That had to be interesting," remarked Sophia at the salon. "You, Brent and the woman who stole him from you, with Ryan caught in the middle."

Mackenzie frowned. "'Interesting' isn't the word I'd use."

"How about crazy, then?" Sophia chuckled. "Not exactly the scenario you pictured when kicking Brent to the curb and sending Ryan to L.A. to make a new life for himself."

"The best-laid plans," Mackenzie said humorlessly while working on her client's hair. "Believe me, in an ideal world,

Ryan would've stayed put and my life would have been a lot less complicated. But it didn't quite work out that way."

"I can see that."

"Getting everyone together in the same room seemed like the best way to tackle the situation."

Sophia snickered. "If you say so."

"It worked," Mackenzie declared. "The problem is solved."

Sophia stopped working. "Yes, I know. Ryan is moving back home with Mommy. But how does Ian fit into this little equation? Or has he suddenly become the quintessential family man?"

"He is what he is." Mackenzie rolled her eyes.

"Which is what? A deejay who may not be prepared to handle a relationship that includes your son?"

One of the stylists, Angelica, came over to Mackenzie's station. "Excuse me for interrupting. I need to borrow one of your brushes."

Mackenzie welcomed the intrusion. "Be my guest."

Angelica opened the drawer and got what she needed. "I'll bring it back."

"Keep the brush," Mackenzie told her, knowing there were plenty of others where that came from in the back room.

"I'm only asking," Sophia picked up where she'd left off.

"You don't know Ian very well." Mackenzie was getting irritated.

"I'll grant you that. But I do know men. I just don't want Ian to decide your world isn't big enough for him and Ryan." Sophia raised a section of her client's hair to be clipped. "Either that, or it's too big for his comfort."

Mackenzie bit her lip. She felt like telling Sophia to mind her own business. As it was, Mackenzie had yet to talk with Ian about this or anything else since the decision had been made to allow Ryan to stay. Between being busy with work and getting Ryan settled, there hadn't been time to discuss it. It would have been nice if Ian had called her or dropped by to say hello. But he had been silent, as though it were too much of an imposition.

Maybe I'm making more out of this than I should. After all, we agreed to give each other space while things with Ryan were worked out.

Mackenzie hoped Ian missed her as much as she missed him. Their passion continued to simmer inside her. She yearned for Ian's sure hands exploring every inch of her. His mouth all over her. But most of all, she missed his companionship and all the time they spent together talking about everything that came to mind. She wondered if what they had built these past few weeks was strong enough to handle any challenges they faced in their relationship. Including the unexpected arrival of her son.

Ian left the station once his shift was over. He planned to spend the afternoon working in his yard and taking Otis out for some exercise. He was nearing his car in the parking lot when a familiar voice said from behind, "Ian, hold up...."

He turned to find Emily ambling across the concrete in high heels.

"Hey," he said routinely.

"I was wondering if you'd be able to give me a ride home."

Ian looked around for her car.

Noticing his roaming eyes, Emily clarified, "It's in the shop. Brake trouble."

Ian cocked a suspicious brow. "How did you get here?"

"My girlfriend dropped me off."

He got a whiff of Emily's potent perfume. Was this her attempt to try to seduce him? She'd come on to him more than once after all. Or was this just an innocent situation where a colleague needed his help?

"Okay, I'll give you a lift."

She beamed. "Thank you so much. I owe you one."

He met her eyes. "Get in."

Five minutes into the drive, Emily turned toward Ian. "So how do you like it now that you've been in Cheri Village for a while?"

"I have no complaints."

"That's not what I heard," Emily said slyly.

Has she been talking to Doug?

"What have you heard?" Ian asked, sounding more alarmed than he meant to.

"That you were having some relationship issues."

Damn Doug for opening his big mouth.

"Who doesn't?" Ian asked casually, trying to play it off.

"Then you do?" Emily persisted.

"Nothing that can't be resolved in time," he said confidently.

"I felt the same way when things became strained between me and my last boyfriend. Only, they went from bad to worse and I ended up dumping him," Emily said, sounding bitter.

"I'm sorry to hear that," Ian offered while keeping his eyes on the road. "But my situation is different."

"Well…" Emily stared at his profile. "Good luck."

"Luck has nothing to do with it," Ian said tartly. "It's all about reasonable people who care about each other following their hearts when all's said and done."

"Spoken like a true romantic."

Ian grinned. "If that's what it takes, so be it."

He dropped her off at her apartment complex.

Emily met Ian's eyes. "Would you like to come up for some coffee?"

"Thanks, but I'll pass," he told her.

"That's cool." Emily pursed full lips. "Maybe some other time, then?"

"Yeah, maybe." Ian kept a straight face. "See you tomorrow."

He watched her walk away, thinking that she was young enough to be his daughter. And though she was nice looking, Emily couldn't hold a candle to Mackenzie in the sex-appeal department. To Ian that spoke volumes. Even beyond that, he wanted to be with someone who could measure up to him intellectually, sexually, and still have enough years behind her to have a pretty good idea of what she wanted out of life.

Mackenzie fit the bill completely. Ian couldn't place a value on finding a woman like Mackenzie at this stage of his life. He wasn't going to give up on her and what she meant to him anytime soon, whether her son moved back or not.

Chapter 21

Ian played the piano with Otis watching and listening lazily. He went through a few songs he still remembered how to play, having fun with it just as he did that night when jamming with Mackenzie.

While Ian recognized his limits as a piano player, he believed Mackenzie could go places. Her talents as a jazz vocalist were that powerful. But that was only half the battle. The other half was the willingness to throw yourself out there totally. Mackenzie seemed less than willing to go to the next level and he respected that. She had her salon and son to consider. Ian was content to enjoy her music at the lounge and with private performances at his house. If Mackenzie chose to focus more on music later, Ian hoped to be there to give his full support. He thought maybe he'd head over to her house tonight to see how she was doing. It would be nice to spend some time with her.

Ian pictured Mackenzie opening her door and the two sharing

a kiss that would leave them both hungry for more. He stopped playing when Otis barked. The doorbell rang. Ian opened the door and his heart leaped at the sight of Mackenzie.

Mackenzie's pulse raced as she looked at Ian. He oozed masculinity in a formfitting, black polo shirt and chino pants. His mustache had been trimmed at the corners but remained an appealing reflection of the man himself.

"Hi," she said demurely.

"Hi." Ian fumbled with his hands while giving her the benefit of a steady gaze.

"I heard you playing the piano and thought I'd come over," Mackenzie offered.

"I'm glad you did," Ian responded warmly.

"I brought this." Mackenzie held up a bottle of white zinfandel.

"Great choice." Ian's lips curved upward, as he reached out to take it from her. "Come on in."

Otis greeted her immediately and Mackenzie allowed him to lick her hand.

"I love you, too," she said to the dog. She gazed up at his owner, knowing the words extended to him even more. She wondered if it worked both ways.

"Why don't I pour us each a glass of this?" Ian offered.

"I'd like that."

Mackenzie followed him into the kitchen. She watched him expertly open the wine and half fill two goblets. All she could think about was getting him into bed and making love. Was he equally hot for her and simply playing it cool, or had the fire been extinguished?

Ian handed her a glass of wine. "How's Ryan?"

"Fine. He's hanging out with some friends. I think they're planning to go see a movie."

Ian regarded her above the rim of his glass. "So did you come to any conclusions on where he'll be living?"

Mackenzie tensed. "Actually, we felt it would be best if Ryan moved back in with me."

"I see."

She couldn't read his expression. "What do you see?"

He gave a half grin. "That you've made a decision. I'm glad. No reason to leave Ryan's future up in the air for any longer than necessary."

Mackenzie felt a sense of relief that he seemed to accept the situation without passing judgment or pulling away from her.

"Since he was having trouble getting along with his dad and stepmom and apparently moved to L.A. for all the wrong reasons to begin with, it seemed like the right thing to do."

"I agree."

She raised a brow. "I know you're not too keen to have children in the picture, but Ryan's going to graduate from high school in less than two years and will probably end up back in L.A. attending UCLA."

"It's fine," Ian told her.

"Really?" Mackenzie asked suspiciously. "I was afraid that—"

Ian stopped her. "Forget what I said before. It's cool that Ryan will be living with you. He's your son and I knew that going in."

Mackenzie felt a quiver of happiness. "All I ask is that you get to know him."

"I'd like that." Ian tasted his wine. "I admit that I have no track record with teenage boys, other than being one myself once, so it does scare me a little. But the thought of losing what we have scares me even more."

She fought back tears. "I feel the same way."

He smiled and took her glass, setting it on the table along with his own.

"I've missed doing this most of all—"

She watched as he angled his head and kissed her. Mackenzie felt a prickle when Ian's mustache brushed against her upper lip. She opened her mouth wider and began to explore his mouth with the same fervor in which he explored hers. She pressed her mouth even tighter against his swollen lips, wanting the kiss to express the depths of her affection.

Mackenzie drew Ian nearer so their bodies closely aligned with one another in perfect harmony. His broad chest pressed against hers, setting her body ablaze. It was all Mackenzie could do not to cry out with pleasure. She could feel Ian's heart pounding in his chest, following the rhythmic pattern of her own. Neither could control themselves as their lips moved zealously in perpetual motion, carrying out their mission of seduction.

Mackenzie ran her hands across his strong back in circular, asymmetrical motions and felt Ian's erection prodding her, eager to be released. The intense throbbing between her legs caused Mackenzie to pant, certain she would come at any moment.

Ian hadn't stopped kissing Mackenzie for a moment, even while they moved to his bedroom. Her soft lips were moist and tasty, covering his with passion. An appealing taste of mint and womanliness left him totally under her spell.

Holding Mackenzie's shoulders firmly, Ian opened his eyes long enough to enjoy seeing her beautiful face so close to his. He loved everything about it—her glowing complexion, her eyelids with coiled lashes, her dainty little nose surrounded by high cheekbones and, of course, those luscious lips that got to him every time.

Ian was happy she'd come over, knowing full well that had he waited any longer, he would have been at her door, ready and willing to pick up where they left off in this sizzling relationship. He recognized what was important in life and right now it was being with this woman. Ian angled his face a little more, kissing Mackenzie with an open mouth to match her passionate kisses. He drew his tongue past her lips and circled her tongue with his.

He sucked her tongue, enjoying its texture and the soft breaths Mackenzie exhaled through her nose. Ian licked the roof of her mouth repeatedly, feeling her react favorably, before refocusing on Mackenzie's lips. He nibbled them gently and found different ways to kiss and caress them.

Ian reached a hand inside Mackenzie's panties. She was very wet, and she moaned as his fingers stimulated her, telling him just how ready she was. He bit back his overwhelming desire to make love to her, wanting to extend the mutual buildup as long as possible.

Mackenzie felt as if she would explode, so intense was their kissing. She yielded to his persuasive lips and wandering tongue while putting everything she had into returning his kisses. Ian's sure hands were all over her as Mackenzie's hands fondled, caressed and stimulated him through and under his clothes. When Mackenzie had gotten worked up to a point where she could no longer stand it, she pried her lips from Ian, wanting much more of the man. The feeling was clearly mutual.

He took her hands, kissing each palm and then sucking her fingers, slowly and deliberately. She enjoyed this and let him know it.

Ian removed her top first. She wasn't wearing a bra, so her breasts were immediately exposed. They were firm and high. She watched his eyes light up at the sight, relishing the erectness of her nipples.

Next came Mackenzie's wedge sandals, then her pants. He brought them down slowly over her hips, caressing her knees and legs along the way. She trembled with each movement of his hands on her warm, moist skin.

Saving her panties for last, Ian put his hand inside, lingering there to feel the wetness between her legs that he had created. Mackenzie sucked in a deep breath and jumped when his thumb crossed her clitoris. She was afraid they might never make it to the bed.

He slid the panties down Mackenzie's legs, past her ankles and to the floor, before gripping her hips and lifting her. As Ian laid her on the bed, Mackenzie lusted for his hard body more than ever before, positioning herself to receive him. He grabbed a condom from the night table and put it on.

"Do you want me?" she uttered, mad with desire as he climbed on top of her and fit between her awaiting legs.

"You know I do," he responded huskily. "I want you more than anything in this world."

"Then take all of me because I'm yours."

Ian gripped her shoulders and slowly wedged their bodies together. Mackenzie cried out, as the moment their bodies connected she knew there was no way she could hold back her release. She spread her legs wider and dug her nails into his back as Ian grunted with pleasure and Mackenzie felt her body envelope him.

"Kiss me," she commanded, wanting to feel their mouths joined when the moment of climax came. Ian found her waiting lips and Mackenzie wrapped her arms around his neck, sucking his lips lasciviously. She darted her tongue in and out of his mouth, tasting him and letting him taste her.

Mackenzie brought her legs up high and wrapped them round his slick back, nearly levitating as Ian went as hard at her as she went back at him. Perspiration flew from one to the other as they kept up the feverish pace, sustaining their love-making longer than either expected.

Ian's chest stimulated Mackenzie's nipples, making her quiver excitedly. He further pleasured her by stroking her clitoris with his hand while he continued his relentless thrusts.

Mackenzie moved her head from side to side wildly and fought to catch her breath, as she reached the point of no return and felt the surge come in full measure.

She moaned loudly and arched her back as a powerful climax overtook her. The sensation quickly spread throughout her body and Mackenzie felt light-headed with joy. At the same time she felt Ian's body shudder violently as he rapidly moved in and out of her. She squeezed him while he was deep inside, enhancing his pleasure and causing Ian to yell out when he reached the point of no return.

Mackenzie softened her kisses as they began to come back down to earth, their wet bodies stuck together, breathing unevenly and heartbeats racing.

"Wow, maybe we need to spend more time apart," she said softly, giggling.

He lifted his head and stared into her eyes. "I think it's just the opposite. We need to spend more time together, so we can do this more often."

Mackenzie smiled, feeling a happy flutter in her chest. "I agree with you. Let's not go on separate vacations any time soon."

Ian grinned. "But taking a vacation together would be nice. I've always wanted to go to the Cayman Islands or Acapulco."

"So have I."

He tickled her toes with his. "Then that settles it. We'll have to make plans to go as soon as possible."

She kissed him and licked her lips seductively. "Sure, why not?"

There had been plenty of exotic destinations Mackenzie wanted to visit when she was married to Brent. But he was always too busy or disinterested. Since being on her own, work had kept her busy. The fact that there was no man in her life made such trips seem pointless to her. But with Ian in her life, Mackenzie truly believed anything was possible now where it concerned romantic outings and good times. And that's when it hit her:

Ian was the man she wanted to be with for the rest of her life.

Chapter 22

On Sunday Mackenzie was in the backyard working in her garden while Ryan watered the lawn. He threatened to turn the water on her, but she gave him one hard look of warning and he backed down. Mackenzie chuckled. She was happy to have him home to help out and to be able to keep an eye on him. He seemed to be readjusting to life back in Cheri Village with no problem. With school due to start in a week, Mackenzie wanted Ryan to focus on keeping his grades up so he could attend any university he wanted to.

Mackenzie gazed over at Ian's house. He was inside with Otis, probably working out. Or maybe he was still recuperating from their marathon sexual escapade the day before. Mackenzie's body was still sore from flexing itself into various new angles and positions. But with Ian she'd learned to never say never. Mackenzie was certain that theirs was a match made in heaven, or in the bedroom, at least.

Ultimately what she wanted most was a ring on her finger and the blissful feeling of spending the rest of her life with the man she loved. But Ian and Ryan still hadn't bonded and Mackenzie didn't want to get her hopes up. She turned her attention back to the garden. She had replaced the plants Otis had gotten into and added scorpion orchids and lavender mountain lilies to her collection. Next year she hoped to expand further with scented geraniums and trumpet honeysuckle, the latter known to attract hummingbirds.

"Good morning."

When Mackenzie recognized the unmistakable sound of Ian's voice, she turned and saw him standing at the fence that separated their yards, a basketball in hand. He had a wide grin on his face, like the cat that swallowed the canary. Mackenzie's heart fluttered as she considered a likely reason why, with thoughts of their intense lovemaking still very much on her mind, as well.

"Hello," she said, lifting her dirty gloved hand for a tiny wave.

"I see you're at it bright and early."

"That's the only way to tend to a lawn and garden."

"You'd know better than I would," Ian said with a smile.

"I'll be happy to give you a few more pointers anytime." Mackenzie grinned.

"I'll keep that in mind." Ian looked over at Ryan. "What's up?"

Ryan continued to water the grass but looked Ian's way. "Not much."

"You play ball?"

"Yeah, some."

"Care to go for a little one on one?"

Ryan lifted a brow. "You mean now?"

"Sure, why not?" Ian gazed at Mackenzie. "Unless your mother objects?"

Mackenzie had no objections and welcomed the opportunity for them to get to know each other.

"Go right ahead," she told Ryan.

"But I'm not finished with the lawn."

"I'll water the rest."

He smiled and faced Ian. "Be right over."

"Cool. And bring your best game. You'll need it."

Ian gave Mackenzie a sexy wink. She hit him back with a half smile. Now it was Ryan's turn to fend for himself. She saw it as a big step forward for the two most important men in her life.

Chapter 23

Ian greeted Ryan with a friendly pat on the shoulder and Otis welcomed him, too, by barking and jumping up on Ryan playfully. Ryan seemed to take it in stride, maintaining his balance and showing no fear of the dog. This impressed Ian as much as Mackenzie had in quickly warming up to Otis. He was starting to think that maybe everything could work out and the four of them—Ian, Mackenzie, Ryan and Otis—could be one big, happy family.

But Ian still wasn't too sure about being a father figure for the first time. What if he failed miserably? Would Ryan resent his advice? And his role in Mackenzie's life?

Ian pushed aside his qualms. He was certainly willing to put forth the effort for Mackenzie's sake. He knew how much this meant to her and, as the woman Ian fully intended to make a future with, he would do whatever it took to stay on track.

He tossed Ryan the ball. "Let's see what you can do."

Ryan grinned. "Yeah, okay."

He dribbled the ball a couple of times, stopped and took a jump shot. The ball swished through the net.

Ian chuckled. "That's pretty good for a start."

Ryan tossed the ball back. "Let's see what *you've* got."

Ian dribbled and tried a hook shot that fell short. "Just getting warmed up," he promised.

Ryan tracked down the ball. "So are we going to play or what?"

Ian smiled. He liked this boy's spunk. It reminded him of himself at that age.

"Take it out of bounds," he told him. "First to twenty-one wins."

As he tried to keep pace with Ryan, Ian had almost forgotten what it was like to be young and have endless energy and jumping ability. Ryan worked his way around him for a layup, nearly dunking the ball.

"Obviously you inherited your talent from your mother," Ian said, sucking in a deep breath.

"Yeah, I guess so."

"She told me you're thinking about attending UCLA?"

"Yeah, maybe," Ryan offered somewhat reluctantly.

"It's a good school. What will you major in, basketball science?" Ian joked.

Ryan flashed his teeth. "Probably architecture or urban design."

"You can't go wrong with either of those."

Ryan drove the ball and went for a layup. Ian blocked his shot and grabbed the ball. "Stay away from the hole," he joked.

"You got lucky," Ryan said.

"Think so, do you?"

"Yeah."

"Well, let's see if I can keep it up." Ian backed Ryan down and outjumped him for an easy layup.

"Good shot," conceded Ryan, catching his breath.

"Not bad for an old man." Ian was grateful for the workout and hoped they could play more often.

Ten minutes later they were on Ian's porch drinking sodas while Otis slept by Ian's feet.

"Do you like to fish?" Ian asked Ryan.

"I guess."

"Bowl?"

"A little."

"Great." Ian smiled over his bottle. "Maybe you and I can do something like that one of these days."

Ryan shrugged. "You don't have to be nice to me just because you like my mom, you know."

"True. But since we both care about each other, it would be easier for everyone if we got along. Don't you think?"

He nodded. "Sure."

"I know things were tough for you out in L.A.," said Ian, figuring he might as well see if he could get him to open up a bit more.

Ryan sipped his drink. "Not everything. I liked the friends I made."

"What about your home life?"

"It was okay. But I didn't always see eye to eye with my stepmother. And my father usually took *her* side."

"I know what you mean."

Ryan's brows rose. "You have a stepmother?"

Ian leaned back in his wicker chair. "No, but I had a best friend who definitely had the stepmother from hell."

Ryan grinned. "How did he deal with it?"

"He just did all he could to keep from butting heads with her. Sometimes it worked, other times he had to face the music."

Ryan pursed his lips. "So you're saying you think I shouldn't have left?"

"Not at all," Ian said carefully. "You did what you needed to do. And it worked out right. I know your Mom is glad to have you back. So am I."

Ryan smiled. "Thanks."

Ian smiled back. For the first time he realized that it might not be a bad thing to become a parent. Ryan seemed amenable to having another parental figure in his life.

Ian was beginning to like the idea of becoming a husband to someone as wonderful as Mackenzie and getting Ryan as part of the bargain. Ian eyed him. "What do you say we have a rematch?"

Ryan smirked. "I'm game if you think you can handle it."

"I can't believe Ryan's living with you again," Estelle said at the gym.

"Well, believe it, because it's true," Mackenzie said, perspiring next to her on a treadmill.

"So, how has the adjustment been with having him home?"

"We're starting to get used to each other again," Mackenzie said. "It'll take some time."

"I thought you wanted freedom?"

"I just wanted what was best for Ryan. But things happen."

"Right, like when a husband goes after anything in a skirt and breaks up the family, leaving the wife to pick up the pieces and glue everything back together."

Mackenzie wiped her brow. "Well, I'm just trying to do what's right for everyone," she stressed.

Estelle took a generous gulp of water from her bottle. "Yeah, I get it. Don't worry, I won't mention Brent anymore. Not with Mr. Neighbor Deejay in the picture." Estelle looked at her. "I take it he still is?"

Mackenzie smiled, thinking about the last time they made love. Her body tingled. "Very much so."

"How are he and Ryan getting along?"

"They're still feeling each other out, but I'm pretty sure it will work out in the end."

"Good. Not all men will do the right thing when kids suddenly become part of the equation."

Mackenzie sighed. "Don't I know it."

"Didn't you say Ian has no kids of his own?" Estelle asked.

"Not that he knows of." Mackenzie gave her a teasing smile.

"Maybe that will change if you play your cards right."

"Maybe," Mackenzie said dreamily. She could picture Ian as a father, even if it was something he'd initially shied away from.

"So am I ever going to meet Ian?" Estelle continued to jog on the treadmill. "Or are you keeping him from your friends— even the happily married ones?"

"You don't need an appointment to stop by my house," Mackenzie countered, knowing full well that Estelle had made a conscious choice to stay away after Mackenzie's divorce. "Ian only lives a few feet away, so we can visit him anytime."

"You made your point." She wiped sweat from her fore- head. "Sorry I haven't dropped by lately. Between trying to keep up with Talbot and going back to school, there just doesn't seem to be enough time in the day."

"I understand."

Mackenzie also had time management issues these days, between keeping up with two jobs, her relationship with Ian and now Ryan's arrival back home. One thing that wasn't a concern was keeping up with Ian in the bedroom. If anything, he had to keep up with her, and he seemed to love every minute of it. Mac- kenzie wondered if they would be able to sustain that frenetic pace. Had they even scratched the surface of how far their sexual imaginations could carry them? She blushed at the thought.

"We should all go out to dinner," Estelle suggested. "I'm sure Talbot would love to pick Ian's brain about classic and contemporary jazz."

"That sounds great." Mackenzie measured her breathing. "Ian seems to have no shortage of views on the subject."

"I'll call you next week to set it up. Is it pretty serious between you two or what?" Estelle stepped off the treadmill. "Is there a possibility we could be hearing wedding bells in the near future?"

Mackenzie had expected the question might come up. That didn't necessarily make answering it any easier. She and Ian hadn't discussed their feelings for each other, much less marriage.

"Yes, it's serious," Mackenzie allowed, drying her face. "How serious...we'll just have to wait and see."

"Hmm...sounds like there's hope for better days to come."

Mackenzie beamed. "They're pretty good right now."

"I can see that," Estelle said. "Good for you. Why should Brent be the only one to find someone else?"

"Who said he should?"

"Not me. You've got so much going for you, it was just a matter of time before Mr. Right came knocking."

Mackenzie laughed. "Actually I was the one who knocked on his door first, as I recall."

Estelle smiled. "Bet it didn't take long for him to get the hint and follow suit."

"Not long at all."

"I'll bet you two are moving back and forth between households like two lovebirds, singing your own brand of music."

Mackenzie tossed her head and chuckled. "I can't deny that."

"I didn't think so." Estelle touched her hand. "Look, whatever happens, I just want you to be happy."

Mackenzie gave her a hug. "And I want the same for you."

"I know, and I love you for it."

Mackenzie held back her emotions, but she was glad to know she could count on her friend to be there. She believed the same was true for Ian, giving her even more to look forward to.

Ian went to the Deer Lounge on a night Mackenzie wasn't there. He was meeting Julius for a drink and taking time to assess his life and love with a friend. Ian had gone through half of his mixed drink when Julius showed up.

"Sorry I'm late. Yasmine called me home for some important news. She's pregnant!"

"Congratulations," Ian said, standing to shake his hand. He assumed this was good news to Julius.

"Thanks. We've been trying to get pregnant for a while now. I'm glad it finally happened."

"So you're ready to ease your way into fatherhood?"

Julius laughed. "I'd better be. In less than nine months I'll probably be changing dirty diapers, rocking the cradle and what have you."

Ian tried to picture Julius taking care of a baby. "That should be interesting."

"Guess I'm settling down and trying to make my woman happy."

"Yeah, that's what it's all about these days."

They sat at the table.

Julius ordered Ian a second drink and one for himself. Soft jazz was being piped through the speakers. The drinks came as the conversation shifted to Ian.

"So, Mackenzie's son is back in town, huh?" Julius noted.

Ian nodded. "Yep."

"And how's that working out for you?"

"So far so good. We seem to be getting along. I haven't stepped on his toes, he hasn't stepped on mine."

"What about for the long term?" Julius eyed him. "We've both been where he is now. Are you going to be able to put your foot down when you need to?"

"Maybe I won't have to. I'm not Ryan's father."

"Never said you were. You could become his stepfather, though. Are you comfortable with that?"

Ian chewed on the notion. "I think so. It's not what I had in mind, that's for sure. But I'll do what I have to do to make this work."

Julius stared. "Then you really are serious about Mackenzie?"

Ian didn't have to think about this one. "As serious as I've ever been about a woman."

"Does she know how you feel?"

"I think so."

"You think, or you know?"

Ian squirmed in the chair. "Well, I haven't exactly come out and said it."

"What the hell are you waiting for—a marching band to lead the way?"

A laugh escaped Ian. "That's a bit over the top, isn't it?"

"Only if you expect her to read your mind." Julius sipped his drink. "Take it from me, man. Women like to know that you're into them. And they want to *hear* the words."

"I haven't heard the 'L word' pop out of her mouth yet," Ian pointed out. Not to say that he needed to hear it right now. He was content with where they were in their relationship, allowing actions to speak more profoundly than words.

Julius chuckled. "You've been single way too long and it shows, whereas I've been around the block more times than I care to admit. But I've learned a thing or two. And I'm telling you, women don't like to put themselves out there first only to find that the man isn't ready to recipro-cate."

"You're saying Yasmine never told you she loved you until you said it first?" Ian gazed across the table.

"That's right. Fortunately I didn't make her wait long. I was crazy about her and I knew she was crazy about me and I didn't want to sit back and watch her walk out of my life."

Ian tried to picture the thrice-married Julius actually being love-struck, apparently for keeps this time around. It made him realize that true love really did prevail after all, and he knew he had to tell Mackenzie just how much he cared about her.

"I guess I'll have to do what I must to keep that from happening."

Julius smiled. "You won't regret it. But I might if Mackenzie decides to step away from singing so she can focus more on building a life with you."

Ian laughed. "I don't think that will happen. She doesn't have to sacrifice one for the other."

"You sure about that? Yasmine was once the world's sexiest flight attendant. Now she's a great hostess for our parties and a dedicated mother-to-be. But I still think she misses her flying days."

"From what I understand, Mackenzie's first husband held her back from reaching her professional potential," Ian said. "I don't intend to do that. And besides, I love hearing her sing way too much to see her give it up. Same goes for her salon. She's invested too much into her business to pull out now."

Julius shook his head with amazement. "You're a better man than me. I'm not sure I'd want Yasmine doing her thing outside the home, especially now that we've got a baby on the way."

Ian snickered. "You *do* know that we're in the twenty-first century, right? Women are capable of doing it all, maybe even more than us guys. That's what I love that about Mackenzie. She's a successful businesswoman, a fantastic singer, a wonderful mother and a sexy-as-hell girlfriend."

"Something tells me it won't be long before you've placed a ring on her finger."

"I've been thinking about it," Ian admitted. He loved the idea of Mackenzie being his wife. He wondered if she was ready for that, or if he should give her more time to be a mother again.

"Well, don't think about it too long," Julius warned. "A woman like Mackenzie who has so much going for her isn't going to wait around forever, you know."

"I'll remember that," he said evenly.

Julius raised his glass. "Here's to neighbors and how they really can change your life."

"You've got that right." Ian laughed and clanked their glasses with his mind set on the most wonderful neighbor in the world.

Chapter 24

"I'm looking for Mackenzie Reese," said the deliveryman.

"I wish I could say that was me," Sophia responded enviously.

Mackenzie came from the back of the salon upon hearing her name. "I'm Mackenzie."

He was holding a vase with a dozen red roses. "These are for you."

Mackenzie blushed and signed for them. "Thank you."

He half smiled. "Better save that thanks for the person who sent them."

After he left, the girls in the salon surrounded Mackenzie, making a fuss over the flowers.

"Gee, I wonder who they're from." Sophia rolled her eyes whimsically.

"Maybe a secret admirer," joked Patty.

"Uh-oh, the secret's about to come out." Lynda made a face.

"Stop it, you guys." Mackenzie chuckled. She pulled out

the card, preferring to read it privately but knowing they would keep pestering her until she came clean.

Mackenzie sighed and read the card.

Hello, sweet lady,
Hope you like roses. I pass by this florist every day and couldn't resist this time. They don't compare to the flowers in your garden, but I hope you like them.
Yours, Ian

"Looks like someone's falling in love," Sophia sang. "Maybe both of you," she added, suggestively.

"Maybe," Mackenzie admitted. She fought hard to keep from crying. Brent had never given her roses. She would always remember this special moment.

"Could a ring be far behind?" Patty wondered.

Mackenzie wondered the same thing but wouldn't get her hopes up. Certainly not here in the middle of her salon.

"You never know," she said simply. "Now everyone get back to work. Our customers aren't paying us to stand around and gossip."

"You're right." Sophia tossed her Senegalese twists to one side. "We can do that later over drinks!"

Mackenzie excused herself and stepped outside to call Ian.

"Hello, gorgeous," he answered, his voice velvety smooth.

"I got your lovely surprise." Mackenzie choked back the emotion, causing her voice to shake. "They're beautiful! Thank you so much."

"I thought they were perfect for a woman who has become the rose of my life and knows a thing or two about flowers."

"Thank you, truly. I can't wait to take them home," she said.

"Or keep them at work, if you like. That way you can think of me every time you see them."

Mackenzie dabbed at her eyes. "I think of you all the time now anyway," she was happy to confess.

"That's just as much as I think about you."

"How did you get to be so special?"

"I think it had something to do with the moment you walked into my life."

Mackenzie beamed. "You just keep pouring on the charm like that and I may never let you go."

"That's what I'm counting on."

Mackenzie felt her pounding heart, amazed at the effect this man had on her.

"Are you doing anything special tomorrow?" she asked.

"Not that I can think of. Why? What did you have in mind?" His voice was deep and seductive, making her heart race.

"I was thinking about going to the balloon festival," she said, assuming he'd heard about the event. "We have one every year. I thought it would be nice to go with Ryan again before he gets too old to want to hang out with his mother."

"Yeah, they've been talking about it at the station. That could be fun." He paused. "Are you sure it's all right if I tag along?"

"Positive. I'd really like you to come. Knowing Ryan, he'll probably catch up with some friends there, so we'll have plenty time to ourselves."

"That sounds inviting."

"Is that a yes?"

"That's an absolutely," Ian said enthusiastically. "I'd love to go to the balloon festival with you."

Mackenzie hung on the word "love," hoping he would direct it at her someday. Meanwhile, she was happy to know her own love for him grew stronger with each passing day.

They arrived at the Festival of Balloons early the next day. It was a perfect morning, with nary a cloud in the sky and plenty of sunshine. Mackenzie was happy to be with the two important men in her life and saw this as another opportunity for them to build a connection.

"It looks like the whole town is here," Ian said, as they made their way through the onlookers in anticipation of the launch of the hot air balloons.

"That's pretty much the size of it," Mackenzie said, her hand clasping his. "We really get into our balloon event."

"I can see that."

"Just wait until you hear the music. It's a nice blend of jazz, blues and rock and roll."

They moved closer to the balloons, which were being initially inflated through cold air from gas-powered fans before propane burners took over. Mackenzie wondered if she'd ever have the nerve to take a balloon ride. Maybe she would if Ian was by her side.

Ian tapped Ryan on the shoulder. "How many of these have you attended?"

"I guess about five or six."

"That's a lot. Are you really into it, or does your mom have to twist your arm to come?"

"Nah." Ryan grinned. "It's cool watching them take the balloons up." He bit into a glazed doughnut.

Ian laughed. "But probably not half as cool as all the refreshments on hand," he said before he took a sip of his latte.

"Yeah, the food's great, too." Ryan wiped his mouth. "Especially later when they have the BBQ cook-off."

"Hmm…I probably should've entered that," Ian said as he considered it. "Maybe next year."

Mackenzie recalled the tenderness of his tasty ribs and chicken. "You should do it," she said. "I think you have a good chance of winning."

Ryan got their attention. "Looks like the balloons are about to go up."

Mackenzie shifted her eyes to the launching area. She felt Ian's arm around her shoulders as the crews of two dozen balloons prepared for the final stages before lift-off.

"It's amazing," Ian said as he watched them rise one by one.

Soon they were all airborne and everyone was cheering. Mackenzie beamed, her arm around his waist. She stole a glance at Ryan, who seemed mesmerized by the balloons floating above them. She couldn't help but think it felt as if they were a real family.

By afternoon they had enjoyed a local repertory theater performance and some arts and crafts. Ian was happy to be in the company of Mackenzie and Ryan at a community event. It made him feel connected in a way he hadn't felt before and seemed the perfect way to transition to what he hoped would become his family.

Mackenzie broke into his train of thought, her arm mingling with Ian's as they listened to some live music. "I'm so glad you came."

"So am I." He smiled at her. "Thanks for inviting me."

"I love being able to experience everything I can with you." She rested her head on his shoulder. "I hope you know by now that you make my world complete."

"Really?"

"Of course. I can't imagine my life anymore without you in it."

Ian breathed in the scent of her floral fragrance. "How does Ryan feel about that?"

She looked up. "Why don't you ask him?"

"I have, but not in so many words."

"And…?"

"He says we're cool," Ian admitted. "But he could be telling us two different things."

Mackenzie licked her lips. "He's not," she promised. "Ryan likes you. He hasn't been crazy about other men I've dated and hasn't hesitated to be up front about it. He sees you as someone who treats me with respect, values my opinion and supports my professional and personal choices."

Ian grinned. "I'm glad to hear that."

"There's more…" Mackenzie widened her eyes. "I actually think Ryan looks up to you and admires you. He likes the fact that you don't talk down to him and you're willing to listen without passing judgment. So you see, like it or not, you're stuck with him."

"I can live with that," Ian assured her. "He's a good kid and he wants to do right by his mother. So do I."

"You're doing very right by me." Mackenzie raised her chin.

Ian zeroed in on her luscious mouth and did the only thing he could under the circumstances. He kissed her soulfully and at length, arousing emotions in him that left no doubt in Ian's mind what he had known for some time now.

He was deeply in love with Mackenzie Reese.

Chapter 25

After work on Tuesday, Mackenzie stopped by a store to buy some sexy lingerie. Ian hadn't specifically mentioned that he wanted her to wear lingerie, as he seemed to really enjoy seeing her completely naked. But she couldn't imagine any man who didn't like sexy underwear on a woman. And what woman didn't feel special wearing some lingerie for a man who adored her?

After admiring many interesting choices, Mackenzie settled on a cute little raspberry chemise, accented with embroidered lace and a black silk bow at the neckline, along with a white V-neck thong-back teddy with a satin lace-up front.

I hope he likes it.

The next day Mackenzie took her purchases over to Ian's house, planning to model them to see which he liked the best. And which one he wanted her to wear to bed that night.

As always, Otis greeted her at the door. Mackenzie was

happy to return his affection, now that she'd become smitten with the Lab and his owner.

"We have become pretty close, Otis, haven't we?" she gushed, as Ian looked on.

"He just might like you better than he does me right now," Ian added, kissing Mackenzie softly on the mouth.

"Oh, you think so, do you?" She ran her tongue across his lips, savoring his taste.

"Sure do." He held her waist, drawing them closer. "Not that I can blame him, since I'm totally captivated by you myself."

Mackenzie grew warm. She met his steady gaze. "I'm just as swept up in you."

"I was hoping you'd say that." Ian kissed her again and took Mackenzie's hand, taking a few steps in the living room toward the piano before stopping abruptly.

She batted her lashes. "Are you planning to play for me?"

He grinned. "Maybe later. Right now I'd like to do something much more pressing than that."

Mackenzie's stomach was churning with nerves. "What?"

Ian sighed, still holding her hand. He kissed it and looked her in the eye. "Tell you that I've fallen in love with you."

"Did you really just say that?" Mackenzie asked, shocked in the best way possible.

He favored her with a serious look. "Yes, and I'll say it again. I love you, Mackenzie."

She felt like melting on the spot. "I love you, too," she confessed, holding his gaze.

"For real?"

"For very real," she replied with a beaming smile.

Ian tilted his head and gave her a long, sweet kiss, which Mackenzie returned with passion. He had finally told her what she had hoped for more than anything, giving her the courage to admit her own true feelings. It was an important first step to what Mackenzie wanted more than anything else in the world—for Ian to be her husband for the rest of her life.

Mackenzie put on the chemise, hoping to arouse Ian to the point that he was crazy with lust to accompany his love for her. After spraying a bit of perfume along her neckline and across her chest, Mackenzie glanced at herself once more in the bathroom mirror. She liked what she saw and was sure Ian would, too.

She stepped into the bedroom and saw Ian lying on the bed naked, legs crossed, hands behind his head. He appraised her thoughtfully.

"You like?" Mackenzie planted a hand on her hip, posing.

Ian smiled broadly. "I definitely like!"

She couldn't resist a big smile and approached him.

The sexiest, most handsome man on the planet was hers. And he cared for her like no one before, showing this through every fiber of his body, heart and soul.

"I love you," Mackenzie whispered, her head resting against Ian's chest.

"I love you, too," Ian assured her as he wrapped his arms tightly around her.

They were going to have a wonderful evening.

Ian was live at the radio station, talking about an upcoming book conference in town and joking about his new garden and green thumb, before playing a stirring Nina Simone rendition of "Someone to Watch Over Me." He used the few free minutes he had to think about the woman he loved deeply and wanted to grow old with.

Ian felt the time was right to ask for Mackenzie's hand in marriage. And he wanted to propose in a unique way that she would always remember. What could be more special than getting engaged live on the radio, with an entire audience of listeners to share in their delight?

As the song started to wind down, Ian's palms grew sweaty with nervous anticipation.

Most men go through this when they're about to pop the question. Right?

He steadied his nerves and focused on the joy Mackenzie had already brought him. Then he dialed her number.

Mackenzie answered on the first ring. "Why, hello there," she said cheerily.

"Hi, baby. Can you turn on the station for a moment?"

"Actually, I'm listening to it right now. I love Nina Simone."

Ian licked his lips. "So do I." *Though not half as much as I love you.* "Well, I want you to hear this next cut. I think you'll like it even more."

"Hmm…" Her voice sounded intrigued. "Go right ahead. I'm all ears."

"Okay, I'll be right back. Don't hang up," he said.

Ian sucked in a deep breath and put his mouth to the microphone. "Nina's one of the best, right up there with Sarah, Ella and Billie. But for me there's someone out there that's even better. This lady sings the standards like a beautiful angel in disguise and, truthfully, I can't get enough of her amazing voice…and everything else about her…."

He paused, noting that Doug and Emily were listening in, as well. This didn't deter him in the slightest.

"It's for that reason that I'm asking her to marry me." Ian choked up. "I love you more than I ever thought I could love anyone, Mackenzie Reese, and I want you to become my wife. If you say yes I'll be the happiest man in Cheri Village and probably the whole world."

He waited for her response.

* * *

Mackenzie was practically speechless after hearing Ian's proposal on the radio. She knew in her heart and soul that he was the person she was meant to be with for the rest of her life.

"The answer is yes, I'll marry you, Ian," Mackenzie cried. "I'd like nothing better than to become Mrs. Ian Kelly."

"You're not just toying with the listeners, are you?" Ian joked. He'd put her on live so she could give her answer on the air. "I'm not sure their hearts could take it any more than mine."

"I couldn't be more serious." Mackenzie wiped away tears. "I love you too much not to want to see us become man and wife."

"You're definitely the best thing that's ever happened to me, Mackenzie, and I'm saying that to everyone who's listening...." Ian's voice broke again. "Thank you for coming into my life."

"I believe it was the other way around," she teased. "As I recall it was you who chose to be my neighbor. Or maybe it was just our destiny?"

She got no argument from him on that one.

Chapter 26

Ian sat at a table by the stage alongside Yasmine and Julius and Estelle and Talbot. They were waiting for Mackenzie to make her appearance tonight at the lounge.

It had been six months since she'd become his wife and Ian had never felt more content. Following the marriage, they took a honeymoon cruise to the Caribbean for two glorious weeks of matrimonial bliss.

Since then Ian and Mackenzie had purchased a brand-new house on the river, marking a new beginning of their life together. Ian accepted Ryan as his son, wanting to make their family complete and pave the way for a possible future addition. He and Mackenzie talked about having a child one day and Ian had grown comfortable with the idea, slowly learning what it took to be a good father.

Ian waited in anticipation while Dorian warmed up the audience with a few songs on the piano. Mackenzie had cut back on appearances at the club lately to focus more on her family and salon. Ian encouraged her to continue singing, not wanting to see Mackenzie's remarkable talent take a backseat in her life. To that effect, he had digitally recorded her music and played it on his morning show to a receptive audience.

He sipped a drink as his wife took the stage.

Mackenzie felt nervous excitement course through her as she approached the audience wearing a strapless ivory satin ball gown.

It was her first time singing at the club in over a month. Would she be rusty even though she'd rehearsed with Dorian beforehand? Her eyes latched onto the table where Ian sat with their friends. Everyone beamed at her, and she gave them a big smile in return.

Mackenzie focused on Ian, the love of her life and her best friend. He gave her a thumbs-up and her racing heart immediately slowed. She took a deep breath and thought about the magnificent life she had. Ian made her whole and was everything she'd hoped for in a man. With an entire lifetime ahead of them, she looked forward to making many memories together.

Bursting with joy, Mackenzie left the stage momentarily and approached Ian's table. She planted a big kiss on his lips, to the applause of the audience.

"I love you, sweetheart," she cooed, practically oblivious to the others at the table.

"Back at you, baby." Ian blew her a kiss that Mackenzie felt deep in her soul.

She waved at everyone and walked back on stage, grabbing the cordless microphone. The jitters were all but gone, replaced by a feeling of peace and comfort, with Ian encouraging her every step of the way.

"Good evening," she said. "Thank you for coming. The first

song I'm going to do is dedicated to my darling husband and it really speaks to what he means to me."

Mackenzie glanced at Dorian for his cue and then turned to Ian.

Her eyes lit up lovingly as Dorian hit the first few notes and Mackenzie began to sing "Our Love Is Here to Stay."

Mother Nature has love on her mind…

Temperatures Rising

Book #1 in *Mother Nature Matchmaker*…

New York Times Bestselling Author

BRENDA JACKSON

Radio producer Sherrie Griffin is used to hot, stormy
weather. But the chemistry between her and sports
DJ Terrence Jeffries is a whole new kind of tempest.
Stranded together during a Florida hurricane, they
take shelter…in each other's arms.

Mother Nature has something brewing…
and neither man nor woman stands a chance.

Coming the first week of May 2009,
wherever books are sold.

KIMANI™
ROMANCE

www.kimanipress.com
www.myspace.com/kimanipress

From perennial bachelor to devoted groom…

For you i Do

Acclaimed Author
ANGIE DANIELS

Feisty Bianca Beaumont is engaged! She's blissful,
until friend London Brown proves she's marrying the
wrong guy. Now Bianca needs a husband to prevent
a scandal, so London proposes. Their marriage is
supposed to be in name only, but their sizzling
attraction may change everything.

"Each new Daniels romance is a true joy."
—*Romantic Times BOOKreviews*

Coming the first week of May 2009 wherever books are sold.

KIMANI™
ROMANCE

REQUEST YOUR FREE BOOKS!

2 FREE NOVELS
PLUS 2 FREE GIFTS!

Love's ultimate destination!

YES! Please send me 2 FREE Kimani™ Romance novels and my 2 FREE gifts (gifts are worth about $10). After receiving them, if I don't wish to receive any more books, I can return the shipping statement marked "cancel." If I don't cancel, I will receive 4 brand-new novels every month and be billed just $4.69 per book in the U.S. or $5.24 per book in Canada, plus 25¢ shipping and handling per book and applicable taxes, if any*. That's a savings of over 20% off the cover price! I understand that accepting the 2 free books and gifts places me under no obligation to buy anything. I can always return a shipment and cancel at any time. Even if I never buy another book from Kimani Press, the two free books and gifts are mine to keep forever.

168 XDN EF2D   368 XDN EF3T

Name	(PLEASE PRINT)	
Address		Apt. #
City	State/Prov.	Zip/Postal Code

Signature (if under 18, a parent or guardian must sign)

Mail to **The Reader Service:**
IN U.S.A.: P.O. Box 1867, Buffalo, NY 14240-1867
IN CANADA: P.O. Box 609, Fort Erie, Ontario L2A 5X3

Not valid to current subscribers of Kimani Romance books.

Want to try two free books from another line?
Call 1-800-873-8635 or visit www.morefreebooks.com.

* Terms and prices subject to change without notice. N.Y. residents add applicable sales tax. Canadian residents will be charged applicable provincial taxes and GST. Offer not valid in Quebec. This offer is limited to one order per household. All orders subject to approval. Credit or debit balances in a customer's account(s) may be offset by any other outstanding balance owed by or to the customer. Please allow 4 to 6 weeks for delivery. Offer available while quantities last.

Your Privacy: Kimani Press is committed to protecting your privacy. Our Privacy Policy is available online at www.eHarlequin.com or upon request from the Reader Service. From time to time we make our lists of customers available to reputable third parties who may have a product or service of interest to you. If you would prefer we not share your name and address, please check here. ☐

KROM08

**The thirteenth novel in
the successful *Hideaway* series...**

NATIONAL BESTSELLING AUTHOR

ROCHELLE ALERS

Secret Agenda

When Vivienne Neal's "perfect life" is turned
upside down, she moves to Florida to take a job
with Diego Cole-Thomas, a powerful CEO with
an intimidating reputation. Vivienne's job skills
prove invaluable to Diego, and on a business trip,
their relationship takes a sensual turn. But when
threatening letters arrive at Diego's office, he
realizes a horrible secret can threaten both of
them—and their future together.

*"There's no doubt that Rochelle Alers is a compelling
storyteller who has the ability to weave romance with
the delicate subtlety of Monet."*
—*Romantic Times BOOKreviews* on *HIDEAWAY*

*Coming the first week of May 2009
wherever books are sold.*

ARABESQUE®

**www.kimanipress.com
www.myspace.com/kimanipress**

KPRA1350509

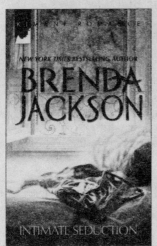